Paul Magrs

Exchange

SIMON AND SCHUSTER

SIMON AND SCHUSTER
First published in Great Britain by Simon & Schuster UK Ltd, 2006
A CBS COMPANY

1 3 5 7 9 10 8 6 4 2

Simon & Schuster UK Ltd
Africa House
64-78 Kingsway
London WC2B 6AH

A CIP catalogue record for this book is available from the British Library

ISBN 1 416 91662 8
EAN 9781416916628

Typeset in Galliard by M Rules
Printed and bound in Great Britain by
Mackays of Chatham plc

Exchange

FOR ALICIA STUBBERSFIELD.

With thanks to Claire Malcolm and everyone at
New Writing North, who commissioned the short story that
eventually became EXCHANGE.

One

They started laughing as soon as they saw him. Simon could hear them from miles away, and he knew he would have to walk past. He would have to brave it out as they laughed their heads off. They'd be jeering and pointing at the tartan shopping bag he was pulling along behind him. It was on wheels and it belonged to his gran.

Why had he let her talk him into taking her shopping bag? Why hadn't he just used normal carrier bags from the supermarket? Everyone else did. Only old pensioners used shopping bags on wheels to fetch their groceries from the shops. Not sixteen-year-old lads. Not unless they were freaks. Freaks who let their grans talk them into using pensioners' bags and who got laughed at in the street by all the other kids.

Kids who don't even know me, he thought. I've only been in this town a couple of months. They don't know anything about me. What gives them the right to go yelling at me?

He knew, though. He knew what it was that gave them the right.

I'm an easy target, he thought.

There he was: down the cheap supermarket, after school, making himself useful and picking up a few bits and bobs for his gran. And then pulling them home in his gran's old tartan shopping bag. The little wheels were trundling away behind him on the wet pavement. He was all buttoned up and mortified in his anorak. He looked like a daft lad, he knew. Soft in the head. And that's how all the kids hanging around the town marketplace saw him.

He sighed and steeled himself to trundle right past them. He tried keeping his head down. If he'd had a snorkel hood he'd have pulled it up.

What did they know? They didn't know anything about him. They didn't know anything at all. Nothing beyond this tiny, run-down place they lived in.

Look at them, he thought. Thinking they were dead cool. There was about six of them. Kids from his year group at school. He recognised a face or two, but didn't want to stare back at them for long. That would only aggravate them. The oldest boy had already left school. He was the hardest one of the lot: wolfish and lean. He swaggered about with a bravado that Simon couldn't help noticing. It really rankled with him, the way that older boy was free to hang around the town centre all day long, if he wanted. He sat on walls, with the others when they skived school, swigging the very cheapest, tartest cider straight from two-litre bottles. He would smoke cigarette after cigarette, fixing Simon with a penetrating, mocking stare whenever Simon passed by.

Rough lads, his mum would have called them. Rough lads and nasty girls. Don't take any notice of them. So Simon tried not to.

His mum had always been relieved that he'd shown no signs of running off and joining the likes of them. Simon was amazed that anyone would ever want to. What was so great about hanging around on the streets? Especially on damp, mizzly November nights like this, when you couldn't even tell whether night had fallen. The mist had settled so thickly on the town. The kids shouting at him seemed trapped in their cone of sickly yellow street light.

And what was so great about hanging around the phone box? That was the saddest thing. There was nothing for that lot to do round here, so they got their kicks hanging around the only phone box in town, in the corner of the market square. It was trashed, of course. Someone had smashed the phone, leaving only the leads dangling. So they couldn't even amuse themselves making hoax calls to the fire brigade or the police or just random numbers. The kids simply sat on the wall beside the box. They smoked and scowled, bitched and slurped at their cider. Then they waited for the likes of Simon to come by so they could shout at him.

Tonight they made a meal of it, because of his gran's tartan shopping trolley. The wheels made a terrible racket on the slick paving stones and he cringed.

Soft lad. Daft lad. Weirdo. Creep.

Maybe these were just the kinds of things they always called new kids. He had only been in this town, living with his grandparents, for about half a term. Seven weeks or something. Hardly any time at all. It was all new and he was still a stranger to the kids in his school. This town was small: stuck up on its hill in the middle of the countryside. Maybe they weren't really used to anyone new coming in. This was just how they reacted. Suspicious. Even slightly hostile. At least, for a while. But that would wear off, wouldn't it?

Fat get. Tosser.

Gradually, he thought, they would get to know him. Slowly but surely, they would come to accept him and he would belong.

Snigger. Snigger. One of the girls – fearsome-looking,

skinny, hair in a scrunchy – popped gum in his face as he went by. He flinched and plodded on, determined not to seem as if he was hurrying. Don't let them see that you're rattled: that's what his dad would have said. That would be his advice. Be brave. Show them that you're just as good as they are.

It was hard, though. Especially once he'd gone by them and he could no longer see them, sitting there on their wall. He couldn't be sure if they weren't coming after him, creeping up, ready to set upon him, once he'd turned off from the market square and down the alleyway that led to the street where his grandparents' bungalow was.

Simon gritted his teeth and kept on trundling. He resisted the temptation to look round behind him. The rumbling of the shopping bag's wheels seemed to fill his whole head.

How did I end up here? he groaned. This lousy place. This rotten town.

Every single thing about his life had changed, these past two months. And none of it for the good.

His mum and dad were dead.

There. He let the words reverberate inside his mind.

The words didn't hurt. They didn't make him flinch or choke up. He could listen to that cold statement inside his mind and know that it was true. Six months after the fact, and did that mean he was accepting it? That he was getting over it?

No. It didn't mean that. That fact was too huge, too weird to take in. Even now. It was still too soon.

But Simon knew that nothing else could hurt him. Not really. Not beside the massive, irreversible fact of his mum and dad being dead. All of his life could crash in flames around him, and still nothing would hurt him or have any impact.

So really, he didn't care what the kids round here did to him. They could yell at him and follow him around down these back streets if they wanted. Even if they beat him up, it didn't really touch him. It was like there was some strange barrier between him and all these new people and this new place. A solid but transparent barrier. OK, so they didn't want him and wouldn't accept him into their school or their town. They thought he was weird and different to them. Well, he was. Simon felt like he wasn't even in the same species as them. As anyone else.

He felt like he was in a different species even to his grandparents. He had moved in with them, lived in their bungalow and, by rights, he belonged to them now. But they weren't quite real to him, even so.

This was his life now. He tried to grasp hold of it. To

know where he was. In this shabby, misty town, Friday teatime, pulling along a tartan shopping bag containing corned beef, full fat milk, sliced white bread, cream cakes. The last was his gran's suggestion, so they could share a proper Friday night treat together.

'Is that you, Simon . . .?' His gran was calling from her kitchenette. She knew it had to be him. There was only him and her and Grandad who had keys to the place. She'd have heard the scraping of his Yale in the porch lock. Grandad would still be down his pub, the Legion, having a couple of pints with his cronies before supper.

Their pattern was set in stone. That was something Simon had learned about his gran and grandad. They didn't half like their routines. Maybe all old people were like that. Wanting to know exactly when every little thing was going to happen. Never any surprises. That's what old people preferred. No shocks, he thought. Weak hearts. They couldn't go round getting shocks and surprises: jolting their poor old hearts.

Living here was like being in a trance. Or being brainwashed. Simon was being forced into the shape of their lives. The repetitious, endless, downward slope of their lives. It was just like the days themselves, growing shorter and darker and less eventful: sliding remorselessly into winter.

He pulled the awkward shopping bag over the doorstep, through the porch, dropping slimy dead leaves behind him.

Inside the bungalow it was too stuffy and warm. His gran liked the heating to be turned up full blast, now the bad weather had started. Hang the expense, she said. Nothing was worse than feeling that misty cold creeping into your bones.

She was standing there in the kitchen doorway, rubbing her hands on a tea towel. She was smiling at him uncertainly. A hesitant, hen-shaped woman in a black knitted pullover. Her hair had been freshly set and rinsed lilac by Rini in the town centre. There were two pink spots on her face from the kitchen heat.

'There you are. There's not every lad who'd go and fetch things from the shop for his gran. Your grandad would never do it. He doesn't even know where the supermarket is.'

'Hm,' said Simon, hefting the shopping bag across the living room and round the coffee table, careful not to let the wet wheels touch the thick pile of the carpet. 'I wish I'd never taken this thing with me. I looked a right idiot. Pulling it along after me . . .'

'Oh,' chuckled his gran. 'It's better than them plastic

bags. They can split and you can strain your back heaving them about. Who's going to see you, anyway? This time of night. Who's going to be looking at you?'

'Kids were,' he said. 'From my year at school. And older ones. They think I'm daft or something.'

'You needn't listen to that lot.' His gran was bending stiffly, emptying the basket onto the kitchen bench. 'They wouldn't help anyone. They'll come to nothing. Was it the ones round the phone box?'

'Hm.'

'Bad ends, they'll come to,' she sighed, examining his groceries, peering over her glasses. 'And their language is blummin' awful, too. Oh! You got the expensive kind of corned beef, did you? And what's this? Help! Luxury cream cakes, eh?'

'You told me to buy them . . .'

'Two apple turnovers and a cream horn. Why, you'll bankrupt us. You'll have us in the poorhouse, our Simon.'

He stared at her and realised that she was having him on. She had caught him out.

'You daft thing,' he said.

She laughed. 'Ee, it's good to see you smile at last. It's been ages. I didn't think we'd see that grin of yours again.' She turned to get out some side plates for the squashy cakes.

'Tell you what. Let's have ours now, shall we? Before your grandad gets back from the Legion.'

If she'd looked at Simon then, she'd have seen the smile frozen on his face. She'd made him self-conscious about it. He felt instantly guilty. What was he doing, buying cream cakes? Talking nonsense and laughing with his gran? What was he doing, fretting about those kids laughing at him? What did any of that matter?

His mum and dad were dead and nothing was real besides that. There was nothing left of them, and yet they were the realest people in his life. Not a single piece of them had been recovered from the wreckage. They were under the sea somewhere, if anywhere. They had fallen out of the sky and disappeared for ever.

These brutal, unsayable facts were all that mattered. Simon found himself dwelling on them and interrupting the flow of every other thought by returning to them. He went over the thought of his mum and dad, under that sea, far away from here, about a million times a day.

'You are grieving, lad,' his gran had told him. Her scratchy old hands on his face. This had been during their only proper conversation about it. It was weeks ago. She'd said: 'You've got to let grief run through its course. It's a terrible thing. You'll get over it. It's the worst thing. But you'll put it behind you. We all will. You've got a new life now. With me and your grandad. You've got to settle into it. And the sooner the better.'

She'd squinted up at him. Her pale eyes were watery and blue. Back then, all Simon could think was: she has lost her daughter. My mum. How can she be so measured and calm about it? How can she tell me to feel, and be so calm herself? There's something either very wrong with her, or with me. I don't think either of us are reacting correctly to this. We don't really know how to deal with it at all.

Simon was used to the smells of his grandparents' house. They had been familiar to him, even before the disaster and his moving in. He'd known them from visits here, from spending afternoons, occasional evenings. Now they had become the smells of home: the fierce, vinegary smell of the gas fire in the living room; gravy and stewed greens; the particular face cream his gran used; the sour scent of beer around his grandad.

And this stale, nearly damp smell in the back bedroom. It was a room his grandparents had never used much. It was narrow, with a candlewick bedspread laid out on the single divan. They hardly ever had guests, so there was an unlived-in air. Now it was Simon's room and even after a few weeks of occupation it hadn't lost that clammy feel. He didn't want to say anything to them about it. Didn't want them to feel he was picking fault.

The room was draughty and clammy because there was a second door, leading into the garage. Really, Simon's room was a short passageway.

He didn't have much room for stuff. Now he realised how spoiled he'd been in his old home, where he could spread out and luxuriate in a proper-sized place. He'd let all his belongings clutter up the whole house and his mum and dad had never minded. Here, he felt chivvied and confined. He found that he didn't want to take up much space. He wanted to feel like he could pack up his few belongings at any given moment, and flee.

So many of his old belongings he'd given away to charity, when he'd left his parents' house. He found that he wasn't that bothered about the bulk of them, anyway. All those dog-eared childhood toys, all those clothes he'd grown out of. What was the point of hanging on to stuff like that? He spent one whole last day in the old house, stuffing things into black plastic bags. He waited for the charity van to come and take them away. He stood out on the driveway with his own belongings strewn about, mixed in with his mum and dad's. All the stuff no one would be needing.

It was a brief visit back to his old life, and his old town. It was only about forty miles from his grandparents' place, but it felt like a different country now.

'Are you sure you want to get rid of so many of your things?' his gran had asked softly. 'Look at this jumper. It's brand new.' He turned to see her rummaging in the bags.

He was keeping a bare minimum, he decided. School clothes (all in the wrong colours for his new school, of course), favourite jeans, a bunch of shirts. There was one shirt he had to hunt out to preserve – a soft, blue denim one with fraying cuffs. Ages ago it had belonged to his dad, and his mum had adopted it to wear around the house, even though it was way too big for her.

Simon took a box load of old photos. He tossed them in loose and then sealed the top with packing tape. He didn't want to go through them yet. It was like these family snaps were pictures of other people, a different family, leading an unfamiliar life.

'You might regret not bringing many of your things,' his gran said. 'You might regret getting rid of all your old life. You can't get these things back, you know, once they're gone.'

He gritted his teeth, almost angrily, and went back to chucking stuff out. Ignoring her. What choice did he have?

The room he was moving to was tiny. His grandparents' bungalow was cramped enough as it was. It was big enough for just them two. What else could he do but get rid of most of his belongings?

One thing – his gran wouldn't let him throw away his books. She put her foot down about that. Soon as she saw that he'd filled six huge cardboard boxes with all his battered old paperbacks, she'd grabbed his arm and said: 'You're not chucking these out, are you? All your books . . .'

He'd already made up his mind. They had to go.

'But you can't!' she gasped. She was scandalised. 'You've always been a proper bookworm. You've been collecting all your books since you were tiny . . .' She opened the flaps of the box closest to her. She scrabbled through the tidily piled books avidly, almost greedily. 'And some of these . . . they're presents from people. Presents from your mum and dad and me and your grandad and oh, Simon . . . You can't just get shot of them . . .' She flipped to the front pages of the top few books, finding the dedications in neat writing on fly-leaves: the Happy Birthdays, the Merry Christmases, the hope-you-love-this-like-I-do's.

'And . . . there's books here that belonged to your mum and dad. Books that go back years . . .' she said, more quietly. 'It's one thing, chucking out their clothes and all the stuff that's useless now. But . . . their books! That they loved, Simon. That you all loved . . .' She shook her head. 'Well, that's like getting rid of them themselves. Their actual memories. All the stories that they ever read . . .'

Simon's face was scalding over like a pan of milk. He found himself snapping at his gran. 'We have to get rid, don't we? There's no point in keeping anything to do with them . . .'

She flinched at his words. 'Ah, don't say that.'

They went quiet for a bit. Simon could have kicked himself, upsetting her like that. She'd sounded disgusted with him. It wasn't just his loss. He shouldn't lash out. Not at her.

'Look,' she said. 'We've got plenty of room. Your grandad won't mind. Look how many books I've got around the place! He won't even notice a few more. Come on. Bring them. Bring them with you.'

'All of them?'

She nodded determinedly, pursing her lips. 'Yes. It seems wrong, somehow, to get rid of books. You need them. They'll remind you of who you are. And where you've been. And you'll need them even more, when everything is changing . . .'

It was true that the bungalow was already quite full with his gran's own books. There were bookcases in each of the rooms, even the kitchen, and the paperbacks were stacked two deep. Some of the shelves were so tightly packed it was hard to prise particular volumes out.

There was a passageway in the middle of the bungalow, and his gran had built piles of books against the walls. Even in the few weeks Simon had been there, those piles of books had started to grow. They were creeping up the magnolia walls towards the ceiling.

It seemed that his gran brought books home every single day. Every time she left the house, she returned with a brown paper parcel. More books, rescued from charity shops, mixed in with the day's groceries. To Simon it seemed like she was smuggling them indoors and adding them to the growing heaps, hoping they were unobtrusive. They were like orphans or lost pets she'd found out in the world, and she was hiding them from Grandad – who, Simon knew, thought the bungalow was full enough.

'The whole place stinks of old paper,' he grumbled. He wasn't exactly overjoyed when the transit van arrived from Simon's old home, bringing the six boxes of novels his gran had convinced him to keep. 'There's that nasty, smoky, woody, dirty smell,' his grandad complained. 'You can catch lice from old paper, you know. Yellow fever. Scarlet fever. Diptheria. Oh, they're dirty old things, books.'

He was sitting in his favourite chair, squinting at them as they unpacked Simon's books in the living room. Gran was tutting and cooing over titles, absorbed in flicking through pages. Simon didn't know if his skinny, sulking grandad was just teasing, or whether he was really annoyed with them. Sometimes it was hard to know how to take the old man. Simon was used to him being a quiet, mildly ironic presence. Living with him, he was seeing a harsher side to his grandad. He had a temper Simon had never seen before. He flew into moods and he could get quite irritated with Simon's gran who, to Simon's surprise, didn't shout back.

That night he erupted all of a sudden when Gran asked him if maybe they could store some of Simon's books in the garage.

'Well, why not?' she asked, keeping her voice steady. 'You're always saying there's too many smelly old books in the house. That garage of yours is standing mostly empty . . .'

Grandad rattled his newspaper crossly, warningly. 'You can't put them in there, because the garage is mine, do you hear, woman? That's the only space I've got. In this whole world. After nearly seventy years in this life, and that garage is the only place I've got to myself. My only privacy . . .' He coughed explosively and glared at them.

Simon could see his point. The garage was Grandad's den. There was hardly anything in it. Just an old armchair and a bit of carpet. Ancient oil stains on the concrete floor. But it was his grandad's own separate world.

Gran had fallen quiet. 'God knows what he does in there,' she whispered to Simon, later that evening. 'I dread to think. But I do think it's mean of him, not to let us use the space . . .'

In the event, Simon emptied the crates of books into his own narrow bedroom. It turned out there was just enough room if he stacked them against the wall to about shoulder height. He had to devise an expert way of piling them up. He layered them like bricks, like a master builder. He tried different ways – the books collapsing and avalanching onto his bed – until he got it right.

He felt like he was walling himself in. Insulating himself against the world, like a Pharaoh in a gilded tomb, embalmed with all his treasure. The pages of the paperbacks started to crinkle with the damp in the air, seeping through the plaster of the walls. But still Simon felt reassuringly insulated and separated from the world.

It felt good to be back in that narrow room, having returned from his grocery trip, changing out of his school clothes, into his jeans and that favourite soft blue shirt. He left the shirt untucked and over his jeans, like he had to nowadays. He'd started putting on some weight recently, from eating his gran's dinners. Her steamed puddings and extra helpings of mash; the doughnuts and biscuits she pressed on him. He was really starting to thicken round the middle and he should do something about it, he supposed.

He felt like the little boy in the fairy tale. Kept captive by the witch in the cottage made of gingerbread. She was feeding him up for the cooking pot. She was blind, the old witch, and, when she pinched his arm to check how succulent he was, she couldn't see he was poking an old chicken bone through the bars. He was deceiving her. No, I'm still skinny. Still skinny as this. It isn't time to eat me yet.

Well. She would expect him back in the kitchen soon. Friday night. She'd be doing her corned beef hash. In about an hour they'd be eating at the kitchen table, shovelling up the delicious, steamy stodge. Drinking hot, milky tea out of mugs. He could hear her now, through the thin walls, clashing the pans about with her usual gusto, and warbling along to some cheesy radio station.

He had maybe an hour to read before they'd want to know where he was. He picked up the next book from the stack closest to his bed. He didn't even look to see what it was. A satisfyingly fat, soft-covered book, the spine bending easily, but not cracking under his fingers. He lay down on the bed, propping himself up on all three pillows. It was a collection of ghost stories he was reading. Just right for the weather, the time of year. From the 1930s. Vintage, twee, gently spooky, and just alarming enough.

He let himself sink into the first few pages, getting his bearings. Slowly but surely, drawn into the tale.

Two

'On a Saturday you have to get out of the house,' Winnie said. 'It's no good just going round all the shops in your own town. You have to get on the bus. You have to get out of town. Go somewhere special. Make the most of Saturday.'

They were catching the bus in the market square at ten in the morning. Grandad was still in bed, but Simon and his gran were togged up in coats and scarves, eagerly waiting for the 213.

'Saturdays are special,' Gran said, clapping her sheepskin gloves together. 'That's when you go out and explore.'

Simon smiled weakly. He was still half asleep really, his head woozy and his mouth too sweet with milky tea. In recent weeks he had been his gran's willing shopping companion and accomplice. They had been on buses going north to the city, and south to smaller towns, then deeper into the countryside to villages hidden away. Winnie knew all the towns in the county, and all the bus routes and timetables. She was an expert in public transport, knowing just where to wait and when. She went jumping nimbly on and off small, short-hop minibuses and then aboard the bigger express coaches that ran up and down the businesslike motorways. Simon was amazed at how adept she was, remembering all the connections and everything, so there was never any vague and useless hanging around on kerbsides.

On subsequent Saturdays through the autumn their journeys took them rolling and twisting through decrepit pit villages, industrial new towns and quaint medieval towns with castles green and mouldy, and tree-lined routes blazing gold and orange.

Simon and his gran always made for the back seat of the bus. It was as if they were pretending it was a huge limousine, driven for just their benefit. As they bounced up hill and down dale the bus was swerving about beneath them, making Simon feel sick the first few times.

When his mum and dad had needed to shop they had gone out in their own car. Straight up the motorway to the nearest mall. This was quite different. This was more like an adventure. He was spending whole days out on the road with his gran.

'Don't you think we should spend our Saturdays with

people our own age?' Simon asked half-jokingly as they clambered aboard, rolling up the long strips of tickets and shunting down the aisle as the bus roared off. Apart from them, it was empty of passengers. A rural service, Simon reflected – probably in danger of being shut down. Then what would his gran do? What would he do? They'd be trapped in that small town at the top of the hill, overlooking miles of muggy green countryside.

Winnie sat down on the velveteen of the back seat, having checked first for any nasty marks or chewing gum. She considered his question, hugging her shiny brown handbag to her bosom. When she thought like this, her mouth would squinch up at one side and her eyes would narrow, as if she was visualising the answer written down in her head. It was the expression she wore when reading, too.

'The thing is,' she said, as their bus took several tight corners round the marketplace and they were forced to lean gently side to side, 'the thing is, Simon, people my own age and your age really bore us. I can't stick other old women my age. Gossiping and showing off about what their kids have done, and what they've all got. And I know that you're not really fussed about young people your age, either.'

'Hm,' said Simon.

'You're deep,' his gran smiled. 'And they don't want to

think about things seriously yet. Well. That's how I was, when I was that young, I think.' She looked at him. 'I wonder if you'd think I was shallow. If you could see me as I was, back then.'

Simon was frowning. It seemed a funny thing to imagine: Winnie as a girl, as a teenager. He had never even seen photos of her that young. He couldn't picture her. She was his gran. She had always been the same. Solid and rather broad in the beam. Wearing crocheted cardigans and woollen skirts. A camel-hair coat. Once, dim in his memory, her hair had been browner and longer. Now her perm was tinted soft candyfloss colours. She had always been older than he could imagine and she always would be. She was his only companion on these trips out, and they had become the highlight of both their weeks. Simon had moderated his usual walking pace so that they could amble along easily together. He sat in cafes with tea and biscuits more often than he normally would, because Winnie needed to gather her strength for yomping round the crowded streets and shopping arcades.

Simon supposed they might look a bit funny going round together. Like Winnie had a toyboy. Like he'd kidnapped some old bird, or was helping her cross the roads like a boy scout would. Sometimes they linked arms, at the end of the day, when she was starting to flag. 'It's the dodging past all the people, all the crowds,' she'd gasp. 'It's different these days. They're all so pushy and aggressive. You've got to mind your feet.'

She wasn't really complaining, though. She loved her Saturdays out with her grandson. By the time they caught their bus home – when it was dark and the queues at the bus station were twenty deep – her eyes would be gleaming with excitement, her arms and legs would be aching and she'd be dying of thirst for a cup of tea at home. Tea in cafes was all very well, but it tasted much nicer at home, after a day of being out and about and amongst life.

The two of them would sit on the bus home clutching their bags of pic-n-mix from Woolies and their second-hand novels bound up in brown paper bags, sweaty and crumpled in their hands. They'd spend the long trip home examining their finds, poring over their brand new battered books.

'We both like the same things, Simon,' she was saying now. 'That's why we both love our days out. It's all tea cakes and Earl Grey and bags of sweets and lovely novels. What more could we want, eh? What more could we possibly want?'

Sometimes it depressed him. Every now and then he'd find himself in a charity shop, standing next to Winnie as she went rummaging in the stacks and racks, and a wave of miserable pity would wash over him. What were they doing in this place, surrounded by the dreary, unwanted, terrible left-over stuff of other people's lives? That smell of old clothes, musty and never quite clean; the saggy cardies and blazers and hot pants and party dresses; the incomplete jigsaws and cracked geegaws and – somehow saddest of all – the discarded baby toys.

His gran's zest for these places was boundless and unquenchable. They were forever in and out of the RSPCA, Cancer Research, Sue Ryder and Scope. Winnie would shuffle in, like she was breezing through Harvey Nichols. She'd ease past the other shoppers – usually fellow pensioners – and she was content just to take her own time, picking through the debris. Simon had to look more enthusiastic than he really felt about these parts of their afternoons together. The saving grace of the drab charity shops would be the inevitable shelves of paperbacks. This was the cheapest way to buy books, and he liked how they were jumbled together: ancient classics cheek by jowl with recent popular blockbusters; westerns and romances; fantasy and stark, searing realism. The erratic order of things exactly reflected his own reading habits and the almost random way he chose what would take up his attention next.

I just drift along, he thought, collecting this stuff together. Any old stuff. No judgement, no value. No real choosing. Just picking up book after book and making my way slowly but surely through them.

Now he was sitting on the bus, and they were entering the suburbs around the market town. Beside him his gran was staring with interest at the new housing developments and Simon was suddenly realising: I'll never have enough time to read all the books I want to. Even if I read every hour, every day of my life and if I took breaks only to eat and sleep enough to keep me alive . . . I'd still never read everything. There were too many novels out there. They stretched into infinity and usually he would find that thought consoling ('I'll never run out of stories to distract me! To fill up my time!') but today the thought of reading and reading and never getting to the end; of never really getting anywhere . . . this thought actually made him shiver. As did the thought of scouring all these charity shops with his gran. They seemed endless, too: every doorway leading to shops crammed with knocked-down, priced-up, second-hand rubbish.

'Have you ever thought of joining the library?' Simon asked his gran.

She frowned. 'What? And drag back books that loads of other people have read?' Such was her logic.

'But everything you read is second-hand,' he said. 'You never buy books brand new.'

She shrugged. 'It's different. I keep them. They're mine afterwards. Oh, no. I've never loved libraries much.'

Simon did. He loved the quiet of libraries. He loved to read without making a sound, without moving a muscle. When he went to libraries he felt tense and alert, like a creature hiding in jungle undergrowth, camouflaged but ready to dash. Winnie, on the other hand, tended to read quite noisily. She crunched apples, crisps, boiled sweets. She commented out loud on the action, letting out involuntary cries and squawks and bursts of laughter. Sometimes she even hummed or whistled as she sped-read through novels, as if providing her own incidental music to the movie inside her head.

'Oh,' she said, elbowing Simon gently in the side. 'We've stopped here for some reason. Something's up.'

Simon had been too busy daydreaming to notice that they had parked up on the roadside, still some distance from the town centre. Peering out, he saw that they were on the long South Road. It was a row of shops that had once been a lot smarter. These days many were closed down, their windows dark or boarded up. Others had become tatty takeaways or sunbed places ('Tan Your Hide!').

'We've broken down,' said Winnie, gathering herself up. 'Look at the driver.' He was out of his seat, looking cross in the aisle, muttering into his mobile. The other few passengers were getting up and starting to leave. 'It's about a mile into town,' Winnie sighed. 'That's a walk we weren't expecting. I'm glad we haven't got our groceries yet.'

Simon was just glad they hadn't brought that tartan shopping bag. This morning he'd managed to talk her out of dragging it along with them.

'It's not your lucky day, is it?' Winnie asked the driver as they squeezed past him. He was still on his phone and he ignored her. 'Bit touchy,' she mouthed at Simon.

Then they were out on the pavement, in an only vaguely familiar part of town.

'Mind out for that dog muck,' Winnie said. 'It's not very clean round here.' She wasn't at all impressed with the South Road. 'Come on, then. We'll never get there at this rate.'

Simon roused himself and managed to get his bearings. And that was when he saw the name on the shop directly in front of them. The windows were dowdy and dim, and at first he thought it was one of the empty, abandoned places. But it wasn't.

The shop's sign was gleaming green and pink. Its

lettering had obviously received a fresh and meticulous new coat only recently.

'What is it?' Winnie asked, as he drew her attention to the shop before them.

'Look,' he grinned. 'Read.'

She squinted up at the sign.

THE GREAT BIG BOOK EXCHANGE.

Three

It smelled delicious inside. It was as if all those hundreds, thousands, millions of pages had spices crushed into their worn grain. What was it? Nutmeg, cinnamon, ginger, saffron. As Simon and his gran moved hesitantly, almost shyly, into the Exchange, he was trying to identify the different scents. There was a homely feel to the place. It was like opening the cupboard where all the spices and ingredients for baking were kept. Smells leading to a million associations and sensations.

And there was coffee and cigarettes, steam and smoke drifting languidly from somewhere deep inside the shop. It was cavernous and they couldn't yet see the cash desk or the owner. They didn't know how deep into this labyrinth of bookcases his centre of operations lay. For the moment, they were hushed and glancing around the narrow space; at the bookcases that lined the walls up to the ceiling; the heaps that lay tidily but unsorted on the threadbare carpet. In the dim, dusty air Simon's eyes were gradually readjusting. There was a single standard lamp, casting a dull bronze glow. It gave a unique ambience to the place. It felt exactly like the wee small hours of the morning. To stand in there, the first room of the Big Book Exchange, was like waking up unexpectedly in the middle of the night. Like sleepwalking, or dozing and drowsily taking one step after another into a room you'd just dreamed up.

Together they embarked on a slow, astonished exploration. Somehow, as they advanced into the next room, and then into the next, almost identical one, they decided that they oughtn't split up just yet. They couldn't stop to browse the tantalising shelves all around them. They had to know the full extent of the Exchange first. It seemed uncanny, as if the shop's chambers might go on for ever, deeper and deeper, the amber light gradually becoming more golden, the ceilings and bookcases growing higher and higher. Simon and his gran crept on together as if scared they'd be split up and lost for ever in this measureless place.

Other rooms branched off into different directions and narrowing corridors. The layout was perplexing. That mattered less and less as they went on, now pausing occasionally to read the subject headings that were written in black marker pen on pieces of card. They were the oddest categories Simon had ever heard of. Stories of Mystery, Fury and Dismay. Tales of Furniture and Geometry. Stories of Exploration and of Staying at Home.

'Someone's got a funny sense of humour,' Winnie said. 'You'd never find anything you were actually looking for, would you?' She kept her voice low, hissing out of the side of her mouth. She's nervous, he thought. He had never seen her like this before. Taking these tiny steps, hardly daring to dart birdlike glances side to side. They made slow, pecking and scratching progress.

The owner of the shop didn't look up. He was sitting at his wide desk in the room furthest back, deepest into the building, reading under a green shaded lamp. When Simon and his gran shuffled in, the owner didn't even stir, he was so focussed on the paperback he was holding open with both hands down on the desk.

Simon felt awkward, as if they had blundered into somebody's living room. He gave a fake cough, to let the owner know that he had customers. The white-haired man was sitting in a bubble of illuminated privacy. Simon turned to smile reassuringly at Winnie, and saw that she had turned away and was scanning through the shelves closest to her. She was walking her fingers along the brightly coloured spines.

Then there was a fourth person in the room. A scowling girl came bustling in from one of the side rooms. She was carrying a heavy pile of art books, which she crashed down on the main desk, puffing up clouds of dust. Her black dress was covered in pale dust. It was a granny's kind of dress, Simon thought. The girl had stark black hair hanging down, with a single electric-blue streak in it. She'd made her face even whiter with make-up. A Goth! That's what she was. That's why she was scowling like that, through all her black eyeliner.

'We've got punters,' the girl said, in a curious, rasping voice. This made Simon jump and turn quickly aside, to pretend that he was scouring the bookshelves like his gran. Still he felt nosy and intrusive. But now, as the bookshop owner raised his grizzled head, Simon himself became the object of scrutiny. The owner's eyes were blazing at him from behind his thick glasses and Simon flinched. Then he coughed again, embarrassed.

The Goth girl sighed heavily and went to sit on a high stool behind what must be the cash desk. As the owner closed his book, the girl was flicking to the correct page in her own and ignoring the customers completely. Almost instantly she had transported herself elsewhere, sitting cross-legged on her stool and holding the novel in front of her face like a mask.

Simon was aware that both he and Winnie were being observed by the owner. Self-consciously he tried to browse.

'Can we help you at all?' the owner asked at last. His voice was mellifluous and rich. Simon couldn't place the accent. He turned to look and the old man was staring at him with all his attention. Simon wasn't used to that. He blushed.

'Oh,' he smiled. 'We're just looking. We popped in on the off chance. We didn't even know you were here. Is this a new shop?'

'No,' the owner said, still staring.

'My gran is a big reader,' Simon said. He didn't know why he was using Winnie as his excuse for being here. Something about the way that old man was looking at him searchingly. It made him feel a bit ashamed and as if he didn't want to be here. He imagined being back aboard the warm, stuffy bus, still heading into the town centre. To the normal shops and the reassuring crush of the ordinary crowds.

Now he was off the beaten track. He had strayed off the path through the woods. He gulped.

Winnie was no help. She was completely tangled up in the books. She had given herself over to her search. Simon could hear her breathing a little more heavily, gathering up a handful of paperbacks, flicking through soft yellow pages.

'And you?' asked the Exchange owner. His voice was sweet and cajoling. He was standing up and smiling wryly. His white hair stood out in unruly tufts. His ears were large and, with the desk light shining behind him, they glowed scarlet. His skin was smooth and somehow thin-looking. He seemed translucent to Simon. Now he wasn't sure he was as old as all that after all. It was true, he was dressed like an old man: shapeless cords, a knitted waistcoat, threadbare slippers.

Simon gave a sudden, stifled gasp. The man's arms. There was something odd about his arms. The way he held them rigid in front of himself. He held out his arms as if he was afraid to damage them.

He stood there, smiling broadly. Simon could see now that the eyes behind those thick glasses were hazel; almost golden. There was a strange, mischievous light dancing there. The man stood about a foot away from Simon, holding out his arms stiffly, and said: 'Are you a reader, too?'

'Me?' Simon said. His mouth had gone dry. 'Oh, yes.'

The owner nodded. 'You'll both be joining, then? Hm? I'll have two new members?'

'Joining?'

The owner's grin broadened. 'Why, the Exchange, of course. The Great Big Book Exchange.'

Simon was silent for a moment. Behind the wide cash desk, the scowling Goth girl tutted loudly once, and tossed her head at Simon's ignorance.

An hour later, Simon had collected up a whole armload of novels. They were in incredible condition. Some of them were as much as fifty years old. Their pages were onion-skin thin but perfect, as if they'd never been opened before. Others were reassuringly fat and their spines were uncracked. His fingers roved indiscriminately across shelves furry with dust. He plucked out bottle green detectives; scarlet translations of European classics; sickly yellow horrors and science fiction with covers that glittered midnight blue. Then the children's books caught his eye. He found books he had forgotten about. The ludicrous adventures of a particular – and very argumentative – clockwork rabbit. He remembered every one of the crisp, gorgeous line drawings. This was the very first book in the series. A perfect copy.

He paused. This shop would be very expensive. The quality of these books was amazing. They were rare. They were far better than the run-of-the-mill charity shop stuff Simon was used to. Maybe they would cost far more than he could afford. In fact, they were bound to. It wasn't every day you found books like these.

He flicked to the front cover of each of the paperbacks he'd rashly picked up. That was where the prices were most often scrawled. Nothing there. Then he turned to the back covers. He blinked. One pound. Then the next one: 70p. And the next: 90p. He was astonished. He had expected at least ten times that amount. Easily. He'd been to antiquarian bookshops before. They'd had books in immaculate condition like this. Some of those shops had even been stocked as impressively as this one. But their prices had made Simon gulp and flush and hurry out of the place. He had been ashamed of even being there and taking the books down off the shelves. They made him feel like he hadn't the right to inquire or to imagine owning books that expensive.

These books, though, were cheap. Obviously they were paperbacks. They'd never really be vastly expensive. Simon was no expert. But surely they were underpriced. There was something else, written in pencil underneath each price. There was another price: 35p, 45p, 25p. 'Exchange value,' it said in each case. He frowned, puzzled.

This was the Exchange.

This wasn't a shop that they were visiting. It worked by rules different to a shop's. Simon and his gran didn't understand yet. It would take them some time to fully appreciate and to learn how to partake in the Great Big Book

Exchange. It wasn't even that complicated. The owner explained it to them very patiently.

'You must bring your books back,' he said. 'You must return them here, to me, when you have read them. You get half the value back each time, and you may put that credit towards your next set of books.'

'I see . . .' said Simon uncertainly. Already he was confused. Any talk of money or figures tended to throw his concentration out. It sounded to him like the owner was promising to buy back the books they'd buy from his shop.

Beside him Winnie had gathered an armload of her own. 'I think I see,' she said. 'So you keep your customers coming back again and again.'

The owner glanced at Winnie and looked her up and down. 'Quite right,' he said. 'Sort of. It's like being in a kind of club, isn't it? Do you see? You'd be involved in the Exchange. You would be included. You'd be reading your way through the many novels we have in stock here. All the great novels in the world. And some surprising ones. You'd be returning them and paying just a little bit of cash each time. But you'll be swapping them along with all the other many customers we have here.'

Simon could have sworn he heard the Goth girl tut once more at this.

'It's brilliant,' the owner said. 'It's fantastic, the way it works. This place is like . . . like a city of books. Or a gigantic brain . . . yes, a brain. And all the books and the readers are like brain cells or synapses or flitting thoughts, passing through and crossing over . . .'

Winnie pursed her lips. 'It sounds exactly like a library to me. But with money.' It was plain from her face that she didn't like libraries much.

'A library!' said the owner hotly. 'Madam, this is the Exchange. It's nothing like a library at all. It's like a very exclusive private club. Why, just anyone can walk in off the streets and join a library. Anyone at all. People who want to come in from the cold. People with no interest in stories at all. Oh dear, no. This is nothing like a library.'

'It's an Exchange,' the Goth girl said in her rasping voice. She slid off her high stool and moved to a silver coffee machine. There, she noisily made herself a strong cup of coffee. She used the smallest cup and saucer Simon had ever seen. 'In fact, it's *the* Exchange. It's the only one like it in the whole world.'

'Oh,' said Winnie, worried that she had caused them offence. 'In that case . . .' She looked at Simon. 'Shall we become members?'

The owner was nodding at them both and grinning

again. To Simon it felt as if they were about to join a secret and rather dodgy society. He wasn't at all sure whether it was a good idea. But . . . the books he had glimpsed, and those he had gathered up in his arms . . . they were irresistible. Long-vanished thrillers and mysteries and meandering sagas. Books that were out of print, obscure, forgotten, never-heard-of. He knew that he would never find them anywhere else. Not in any other bookshop. Not even in the library.

'Yes,' he said. 'I think we should join.' His heart was beating a little harder. The girl at the counter glanced at him. Her heavily kohl-blackened eye winked at him. We're really getting into something here, he thought. Something we never expected to find. Now he and his gran were happily giving themselves up to the adventure of it.

The Exchange owner was delighted at this. He hurried back across the worn, elaborate carpet and set about finding fresh membership cards. They were small, grey, old-fashioned things. He wanted them to fill them in immediately, with their full names and addresses. He asked his Goth girl assistant to find a pen.

Then he prodded the two grey cards across the desk at them. Winnie looked down and found herself staring at the tips of his rather small, neat fingers. She realised that he was holding them very stiffly. Both hands were like that. They were lifeless. Her breath gave a little catch in her throat as it hit her that the man had two artificial hands. She almost cried out but Simon, who had noticed the same thing at precisely the same moment, nudged her silently in the ribs. Don't say anything. Don't draw attention to it.

Simon took up the proffered Biro and the stiff piece of card. He signed himself up for the Exchange, and tried not to stare at the man's plastic forearms as they rested there on the desk before him.

Four

They didn't tell Grandad. It wasn't a conscious decision. It wasn't as if they thought they should treat their joining the Exchange as a secret. It wasn't as if they had done anything wrong, like spending an exorbitant amount of money.

They just both knew that Grandad wouldn't appreciate the tale of their Saturday adventure and the discovery of the place – that labyrinth of novels – owned by the man with two plastic arms, and his taciturn, Gothic assistant.

Grandad wasn't a reader. He would never understand their hushed excitement, their spooked out nervous enchantment. He would think they were silly. He'd be nonplussed as they explained it all: what the Exchange was like, how the owner had behaved, and what he had said to them. The tale would turn to ashes in their mouths. Worse still, Grandad might even ridicule them. Tell them they were getting worked up about nothing.

With that mocking tone of his he might make them feel that the whole escapade wasn't all that important or interesting. What on Earth were they on about? So what?

So they kept quiet about it. They brought the books home, hoping they would go unnoticed by Grandad: Simon adding his to the heaps by his bed; his gran keeping hers safe on her bedside table.

It was frozen, foggy and dark by the time they returned home that night. All Grandad was really bothered about was sending Simon to fetch back fish and chips from the chippy in the town square. Simon went gladly, clutching a tenner, into the silvery dark. He was starving by now, thinking of chips and scraps of golden batter, glistening with malty vinegar. He tried to duck unseen by the kids next to their phone box.

'We saw you! Going out with your granny!'

'She's your girlfriend, isn't she?'

He queued in the fish shop, ignoring them. Especially ignoring the oldest lad, who was grinning at him nastily and wolfishly. He could still see the kids through the wide window, capering about and laughing. He blocked them out. He thought about the long, lovely quiet hours of that evening to come. The first of his novels from the Exchange, open on his lap. The gas fire blazing away, and some old record of his grandparents' crackling on their ancient stereo. They still had their old vinyl and they favoured syrupy string arrangements of golden oldies.

He would start on the first of his Exchange novels. He had to. He had to get them read. They had to go back next Saturday. That was the bargain.

The first of his novels was – it said on the back – a classic of Fifties existentialism, set in Paris. He didn't know what that meant exactly, but judging from the deliciously lurid cover illustration it involved people in grimy little cafes, talking about life and how hopeless it was; being very glamorous and smoking lots of cigarettes.

He couldn't wait to get home with his steaming parcels of chips and battered cod. He looked forward to getting through what had become their various Saturday night rituals: lottery on the telly after the fish and chips, then a pot of tea and Madeira cake. And then Grandad turned DJ, opening up the wooden cupboard and flipping through the records, as Winnie and Simon settled down to their reading for the rest of the weekend.

Simon had learned to grit his teeth and simply get through his time at school. He kept his head down and thought himself lucky if he got through a day without getting punched or yelled at or deliberately tripped up in the dark, crowded corridors as the kids went from room to room, bells ringing in their ears.

'You're wishing your life away,' his gran would say, when he counted down the days each week. 'You should enjoy your time at school. Best days of your life, you know – what they say is true. All too soon you'll have to work for your living and that's no picnic. You shouldn't hurry time up, wishing you were older . . .'

Yet that was precisely what he did do. He wished he was older and free to go off anywhere he wanted and become anyone he wanted to be. Like Winnie, his best friends weren't real people. They were lords and ladies in the eighteenth century; they were roughnecks and pirates in the wild west, the untamed seas or in Sherwood Forest; they were exotic heroes in the far future, or they were flashy femmes fatales in a more glamorous age. Inside his head, Simon could pretend to be in whichever company he wanted. He could imagine finally growing up to be anyone at all.

As the day-to-day circumstances of his life closed in around him his fantasies grew more and more elaborate.

To the other kids at school he must have looked furtive and sneaky. Every gap between lessons he was going off to secret spots like behind the sports hall, or the cloakrooms of his house block. There he would read avidly, his eyes darting about shiftily, wary of being caught. He was shifty as a house-burglar, snatching ten minutes here, half an hour there. He faked letters from his gran to his form tutor and his PE teacher, explaining how, due to stress, to grief, to a chronic stomach upset, Simon wouldn't be running cross-country today, or indeed, anything else he didn't really fancy doing.

He schmoozed with the school librarian to get to stay in during lunch hours so he could sit at the polished wooden table in the centre of the room, working steadily through his novels. He could tell that the school librarian was at first pleased to see one of the pupils so keen on reading. And this was the boy whose parents had died in that plane crash. Maybe she was doing a vital service here, she thought. She was doing a good thing, letting him stay in when the school rules insisted that all children should be out, getting lashed by the autumn wind and rain. But after a while she started to fret about him. There was a feverish look to him; in the determined way he sat, as if ready to resist being dragged away. There was a steely glint of obsession in his eye.

Never before had the librarian seen a boy his age reading the kinds of books he did. One day: a tale of partying socialite divorcees in 1960s New York. He read it with the same solid absorption as he did a huge Russian novel from the previous century. With unbelieving eyes the librarian had spied on him tackling that one, just a matter of weeks ago. She had the feeling that if she had given him the local phone directory he would have read it just as happily.

She was wrong there, however. It was novels that Simon liked to read. He could have told her, had she come over and asked. What he read for, purely and simply, was story. That's where he got his kicks. He wanted rich and vivid characters of each and every type and he wanted to find out what they got up to, and what they all did to each other, and behind each other's backs. He wanted to see them set against the glittering, hugely panoramic backdrop of their society and time. He wanted to understand places and people unfamiliar to him. When he read, he couldn't always follow the politics or the more abstruse plots or the more subtle nuances. Sometimes he skipped bits he thought were boring, but he kept on reading for the sake of the characters. For the sake of imagining that he was one of them and finding out what became of them in the end.

He read novels with the same committed interest and zeal as his grandad would watch the evening news. They both had to know what was going on out there, in the world. To Simon, his fictional world was just as real as that horrifying, violent world that his grandad watched and tutted over on the news.

Hiding from the real world. That's what he and his gran were doing. That's what his grandad always threw at them: it was an accusation. It was meant to be an insult. To Simon it wasn't that bad an insult. Not at all. Not compared to some others. He thought about replying: So what? What's wrong with hiding from the real world, then? The real world is a terrible place.

He loved novels because their writers took that raw, nasty stuff the real world was made of, and they fashioned it into . . . something better. Not necessarily something sugary sweet and rose-tinted. But something brighter, maybe, larger than life and more dramatic. Simon's writers recreated the world so that it started to make sense to him. Novels gave him the feeling that there were, perhaps, answers out there somewhere.

His writers made him feel that life was purposeful, happiness possible, and people important.

The news he watched with his grandad each night made him feel the complete opposite.

He lay on his bed, mulling all this over. Suddenly an image popped into his mind. An image of that Goth girl in the shop, perching on her high stool, slowly and deliberately leafing through the pages of her paperback. She was meant to be an assistant to the man with two plastic arms, but she hadn't been doing much assisting. She had looked too caught up in the story she was reading. She had been very cool and aloof. Nothing furtive or ashamed about the way she had been reading. She hadn't looked at all apologetic about it. Once, she had looked up over her book and winked at Simon. He could picture her doing it right now.

Why had she popped up in his mind just then?

Just as quickly, he knew the answer.

She is the same as me, he thought. He smiled to himself. That girl – she's the same. She feels the same as I do, about novels and people and the rest of the world.

It was Thursday night. He still had nearly two full books to read before he was finished and ready to return the whole batch to the Exchange. He would have to crack on. He wanted to go back this Saturday. He wanted to see it all again, to make sure that it was all real. Those books, the man and that girl, dressed in black and perching on her tall silver stool.

Five

He didn't have a regular bedtime any more. Maybe his grandparents thought he was grown up now. They didn't want to come on heavy-handed. They didn't want to tell him he should get a good night's rest for school.

What he tended to do was read in the armchair in the corner of the living room while his grandparents went about their customary evenings. Only when he had exhausted himself, and read himself into a standstill, with the lines of words starting to blur one into the next, would he take himself off to his room. That small bedroom seemed that much cooler, with just a tinge of damp lingering in the walls and the white cotton sheets, as the winter nights deepened.

His gran would always be first to go off to bed, with her oddly formal 'Goodnight, all!' from the doorway. She would be in her dressing gown and slippers, teeth out and holding one hand shyly in front of her mouth. She'd be clutching a book to her chest. She was the first to bed but she was almost always the last to sleep, Simon knew. All the doors in the bungalow were ill-fitting and if there was a light left on through the night, it would seep out onto the small landing. Getting up for the loo or a drink (Simon was a very light sleeper, especially that year), he would see the warm light spilling out of his grandparents' room. He knew she would be sitting up in bed with her side lamp on, her knees drawn up, book resting on the thick duvet. She'd be squinting at the words, ravelling them up through the night.

Next to her, his grandad Ray would be fast asleep. The breath rattling in his throat as he lay there, flat on his back. Gran said Grandad could sleep through anything. He had come through the war aboard submarines, sleeping in hammocks as torpedoes struck. Surely he wouldn't be disturbed by Winnie. She tried to be quiet for his sake. She tried to sit still. She didn't crunch sweets or laugh aloud. It was hard, though, to suppress those reactions.

She did try, though, she told Simon. She didn't want to be a nuisance to Grandad.

Simon watched the old man's face as Winnie went off to bed. Grandad's expression was dark; his eyes glowering after his wife.

'That'll be her, sat up all night again,' Grandad muttered, half to himself, half to Simon. Simon was surprised at the sourness in his voice.

'She's completely obsessed with that book she's in the middle of,' Simon said. 'It's one of the ones she got last Saturday. She says it's amazing because—'

His grandad cut him short. 'Do you know, I'm not all that bothered? I've had about enough of hearing about your books, you two. A lad of your age. And her! She hardly sleeps more than three hours a night. That's no good for her health. And besides, she's neglecting the housework. There's a sinkful of dishes through there that haven't been done. This whole place is starting to feel neglected . . .'

Simon wasn't even used to his grandad speaking to him on a one-to-one basis, let alone getting a sustained rant like this. Complaints about his gran! He was shocked – but thrilled, also, in a strange way. It was true that she had become a bit slipshod in her habits of late. The dishes weren't clean tonight and the breakfast things weren't set out ready on the table. There was a scattering of dust on the mantelpiece and her ornaments. There were bits in the carpet that hadn't been hoovered for days. Maybe she was reading for more hours of the day than ever before.

But was that a problem? Simon didn't think so. He

envied her. At least she didn't have to waste good reading time by going to school.

She only slept three hours a night, his grandad said. Did that mean she was keeping the old man awake? And was she being so selfish and obsessed that she didn't even know it?

'I'll have to say something to her,' Grandad said now. 'I'll have to do something. It's making me miserable, all this. It's like living with two strangers. With two zombies!'

'Are we as bad as all that?' asked Simon.

His grandad Ray looked at him and his expression softened. 'I don't see what the two of you get out of it. Really, I don't. Maybe that's my problem. But – God help me – I can't understand what you're doing with your waking lives. All those hours. I feel like . . . I may as well not be here. Like the two of you are trying to read your way out of this place altogether . . .'

Simon didn't have anything to say to that. He couldn't deny it. He watched as his grandad got up stiffly out of his swivel chair. 'Aye, well. I imagine that you, Simon, really are trying to escape. But your gran . . . She belongs here. With me. Where do you think she wants to get to?'

Simon couldn't tell him. But, oddly enough, he knew. That particular week, he knew where his gran was going off to in her head. He knew where she was imagining herself when she read for those long hours. He watched his grandad shuffle off to bed and he knew that his grandad was irritated with him, too. Simon felt like he had been asked for help and he had refused to give it.

Simon sat alone, staring into space under the tassled standard lamp. He'd do the dishes himself. He'd tidy round tonight. Put out tomorrow's breakfast things.

It wasn't just a vague 'elsewhere' that his gran had been escaping to that week. It wasn't just some imaginary place. She had explained it to Simon earlier that day – teatime on Friday. She had been delighted, surprised and bleary-eyed as she had told him.

Winnie had been escaping into her own past.

'This one. Here. I knew straight away. I knew as soon as I picked it off the shelf last Saturday. Back at the Exchange. I mean, of course, I recognised the name. She's a famous writer. But I didn't know about this particular novel. Or what it was about.'

Winnie was gabbling slightly. It was a habit Simon had too, when he got carried away about something.

They were having tea, sitting at the colourful oil cloth on the kitchen table. The fat novel in question lay between them, amongst the side plates and the crumbs of flaky pastry.

'Hang on,' Simon said. 'Let's get this straight. You reckon that you know her?' He touched the book's faded, battered cover. In all honesty, the book looked a bit tacky to him. Not that he minded a bit of tackiness! But you had to draw the line somewhere, didn't you? And this was one of those really tawdry, supposedly heart-warming romances all about love-against-the-odds and extreme poverty. On the front cover was a badly drawn street of back-to-back houses, urchins in the background, and in the foreground, on the cobbled street: a woman in a flowery dress. The title was embossed in gold foil – *Mary and Agnes* – and the author's name, in even larger lettering: Ada Jones.

Simon knew the name. Ada Jones was a local legend.

'You never mentioned this before,' he said. 'Ada Jones is really famous. Worldwide! How do you know her?'

His gran blushed. 'It's not the kind of thing you like to talk about, is it? People will think you're showing off. It doesn't count for anything, anyway, because I haven't seen her in years. Decades. She wouldn't even recognise me nowadays.'

'How long is it? Since you last saw each other?'

His gran shrugged and puffed out her lips. 'Before you were born. Before your mum was born, even. Maybe it was just after the war. I can't remember exactly. Well, she went off down south. She got married down there. Married a doctor. She never came back to our town. She forgot all about us lot. That's what I thought.'

'That's a proper rags-to-riches story.'

'At least,' his gran smiled oddly, 'I always assumed that she'd forgotten about us and about me. Until I started reading this.' She tapped the book softly.

'It's about you?'

She shook her head modestly, looking slightly confused. 'Yes. I don't know. Bits of it, perhaps. It's about two girls growing up in a street very like the one where we grew up . . . me and Ada. It's all very like. It's just how I remember it.' Her voice was going a bit shaky. 'And I thought – so you did remember, Ada. You remembered me. You see, I thought she'd gone off and made this grand success of her life and she'd left us all behind. Turns out that wasn't really so.'

'And it's definitely you? It's about you?'

'This was her first book. The first one she ever published. Back in the 1950s. I don't know why I never read it. I've only looked at a couple of hers, over the years. She must have written about forty of the things. I was envious, I suppose.' Winnie stared past Simon, through the Venetian blinds and out beyond the small front yard. 'I'm a silly woman. Here was my story, all along. My own childhood and when I was a girl. They've been in a book. All that time. Only I never found them. But I found them in the Exchange, though. First book I laid my hands on. It just about fell off the shelf into my hand. Weird, isn't it? I suppose I was meant to find it, just at that moment, after all that long while.'

'Have you finished it?' Simon flicked through the book, riffling the pages softly. There was nearly a thousand of them.

'Not yet.' She sniffed. 'I've been reading like a maniac. Getting to know Ada again. Getting to know me again. As we both were, back then. It's been wonderful. And frightening. And . . . I want to get to the ending. To find out how we end up. To see if Ada lets us be happy at the finish. And yet I'm also dreading it. Of course I am.'

'Why?'

His gran looked at him steadily. 'Because I already know the ending, don't I? The two girls get split up for ever. Childhood ends. Youth ends. Real life begins. Oh, do I know how the rest of the story goes . . .' She sounded bleak. Her tone had gone dead. 'So of course I don't want to finish it.'

'He'll want it back,' Simon said suddenly. He blinked. What had made him say that? Of all things?

'Who will?'

'The man in the Exchange,' Simon said softly. 'He made us promise, didn't he? About returning the books for credit.'

She shook her head firmly. 'I couldn't give this back. I'm sure he'll understand. This isn't the kind of thing you can just give away again.'

Simon wanted to say to her: just a week ago you didn't even know that book existed.

But there was still that distant, slightly hurt look in his gran's eye and so he didn't go on.

At first Ada Jones was just one of the dirty kids next door.

She was one of the youngest belonging to the new, rough family who made so much noise and who'd already started fights with the neighbours. The husband was a young bruiser with a chip on his shoulder. His wife looked like a common slut, Winnie's mum had said. Also: the inside of their place was infested. It was a proper disgrace. They'd ruined it already and God knows how many they had living there. It was a proper slum indoors and they were bringing down the tone of the street. But – Winnie's mum went on – her heart bled for the younger ones. The babies. They looked filthy. They were never even properly dressed. One of the toddlers was out playing in the street, wearing just one sock and an old vest.

Ada Jones was terribly thin. She was just about white in complexion. The bones of her skull were sticking out in her face, so that, when her head popped up behind the garden wall, the day they first met, Winnie just about yelled out in horror. Ada's hair was lank and pale. Her eyes, though – they were bonny. Sort of minty green, Winnie thought. They seemed to change, according to her mood.

And Ada's moods changed quite often, quite dramatically. She could be teasing, laughing and joking one minute – and then she could fly into a temper. She'd go all offended and aggrieved, lashing out with her stick-thin arms and legs. Utterly fearless, she'd give anyone a belting, if provoked. As they went on to become friends, Winnie's role was most often having to bail Ada out of the trouble she got herself into.

Then, from temper, Ada's moods could swing back down into miserable self-pity and wheedling: 'You're still my friend, aren't you? You don't hate me, do you? Do you?' Even though Winnie knew Ada was a great one for putting on an act, she was always taken in. Even though she knew she was being manipulated by her tiny, pale, weedy friend, she loved her and didn't mind.

Ada was a slum kid. A street kid. A backyard waif. She was helping to drag up her brothers and sisters, and to make sure that they all survived. If she lashed out occasionally, so what? If she didn't have perfect manners, or got a bit hot-tempered or dreamy sometimes – who cared?

Winnie and Ada were best friends and it started the day Ada hopped up over the wall separating their two backyards and introduced herself by quizzing Winnie. She asked her the nosiest, most intrusive questions Winnie could imagine.

'Is your father dead, then? Or did he just run away with a fancy woman? Who's the old bird you've got living with you? She looks horrible. What does your mammy do? I've seen her go off first thing in the morning. Is she cleaning some-where? Is she nice? She's got a kind face, I think. Does she hit you ever? Have you got bruises? I have. Look at these! Look!'

Winnie had been pegging out her mother's washing and she was shocked by Ada Jones. Right from that first moment. No one ever talked like she did. Certainly no one that Winnie knew. She watched in calm astonishment as Ada struggled over the brick wall, smudging green mould on her already dirty frock, and came to show off her bruises. Livid, purple-yellow bruises up the backs of her arms and legs. They were the colours of pansies, Winnie thought.

'My mammy can be proper nasty,' Ada said, almost proudly. 'It's not really her. It's all the gin. And the awful life.

And all us kids pulling at her. She's not really bad, not when she's not been boozing. So I should forgive her, you see.'

Winnie was gobsmacked. This was shocking talk. And the girl wasn't even whispering. She wasn't hissing out of the corner of her mouth. Ada spoke loudly and clearly – a voice much too big for this tiny little body. Winnie was to get used to this. Ada simply didn't care who heard what she had to say. She liked to broadcast all her business; all her thoughts and opinions.

'I've got the gift of the gab,' she told Winnie. 'Why shouldn't everyone hear what I've got to say? I'm as good as anyone. I've got nothing to hide.'

'Sssh!' Winnie gasped, appalled, clutching the peg bag to her stomach as she started to laugh.

'I don't care,' shouted Ada. 'I'll tell the whole world anything it wants to hear. Hear that? Hear the echo? My mammy's got too many kids! She drinks gin when she can get it! She's up in her bed still, right now! With a great big raging headache!' Ada pointed up at the back window, where the curtains were pulled against the bright morning. 'I don't care who hears!' Ada shrieked. 'Let them all listen!'

Winnie bit her lip, delighted by all of this.

'You're Winnie, aren't you?' Ada asked.

Winnie nodded.

Ada studied her face carefully. 'I've decided that you've got to be my friend. No ifs, no buts. It's what I've decided and you've got no choice in the matter.'

'All right . . .' Winnie stammered.

'And I mean friends for life, you know. When I make up my mind, I really mean it. And I mean we'll be friends when we're old, old ladies and we're both probably still living next door to each other, like this.'

Winnie nodded.

'Not round here, though,' said Ada. 'We won't be living round here.'

'Where then?' Winnie hardly understood what Ada meant. At seven, Winnie couldn't really picture anywhere that wasn't round here: this street amongst so many other, similar streets, leading down to the docks and the silver-brown mass of the slow-moving river. To her, the 'world beyond' meant only the docks and the great hulks of half-finished ships, stilled in the water like vast wedding dresses with pins sticking out. Waiting to sail out to the sea and over the edge.

'We'll be somewhere else,' Ada said. 'Somewhere posh. The place we both deserve to be.'

Six

This time, the man who owned the Book Exchange didn't seem as friendly.

Last week he had been almost effusive, jumping up to congratulate them and to give them their special membership cards. This week it was all quite different.

When Simon and Winnie entered the Exchange, everything seemed at first exactly the same. The autumnal gloom outside; the timeless, amber glow indoors. The scents of old paper, woodsmoke and faintly exotic spices were even more marked and they had both sighed, without even knowing it – letting the stresses of the week drop away from themselves as they advanced into the Exchange. Much more sure-footed now, the two of them. They knew their way about, inside here. There was nothing to be wary about.

They belonged here. That was how they felt, as they

made their way to the room in the middle of the oddly-shaped building. Again, there didn't appear to be any other customers peering and shuffling through the orderly stacks and this only heightened their feeling that this was a place meant solely and especially for them.

Both Simon and Winnie were carrying parcels of books with them. Simon had brought last week's books back. Winnie had brought some others. Three unwanted novels she hadn't much liked. Three novels she'd had for ages. She hoped that the Exchange owner would accept them in lieu of the Ada Jones novel, which she had decided she would very much like to keep.

'I know it goes right against the rules of the place,' she'd said to Simon on the bus.

'It does,' he teased. 'This is the first time you've been and you've broken the rules already.'

'But I can't give that book back. You know why . . .'

'You really like it that much?'

Her face clouded. 'It's not a question of liking it. It's my life. That's what's in that book. I'm sure if I explain it to him he won't mind. He'll take these sloppy romantic novels instead. I've done with them. And they're in much better condition than this old Ada Jones . . .'

Winnie was wrong, though. The Exchange owner

wasn't at all impressed with her, or what she was intending to swap.

'What's this?' he sighed, prodding her gaudy romances with the tips of his plastic fingers. His voice was very distant and cold. Winnie and Simon had known, as soon as they'd entered his inner sanctum, that his mood was different this week. The whole atmosphere of the place was changed. He really was like a tetchy spider, sitting in the dead centre of his web; setting off vibrations with the tiniest of gestures.

The two of them stood there, shame-faced. They had got it wrong on only their second visit.

'Tell me what this is,' he said again, coldly, looking up at Winnie.

She tried to explain. 'I've brought back two of the books I took from here last week. And I've replaced the third one with these other romances. I hoped you'd take them instead of the Ada Jones novel I found here. In exchange, if you like.' She gave a very uneasy, embarrassed laugh. 'This is the Exchange, after all, isn't it?'

He snorted at her words. Utter disgust, Simon thought. Then Simon was aware of the Goth girl, sitting on her high stool at the cash desk. He hardly dared look at her, though he knew she was watching this little scene. He darted a quick glance at her. She was watching with great interest – an expression of pity on her white face. Simon blushed as she caught his eye and smirked at him. She was smirking at his gran's bumbling stupidity.

The Exchange owner said: 'These are just trash.' He shoved the silly romances back at Winnie. 'I will not have trash like that clogging up the shelves of my Exchange.'

Winnie tried to stick up for herself. 'But you aren't snobbish. You stock all kinds of books here. Not just posh ones. You've got westerns and horror! You've got other romantic fiction . . . I've seen all sorts of things here . . .'

The man's almost translucent skin was turning scarlet with pent-up rage. That wayward hair of his seemed to be bristling. 'I do not stock trash, madam. I stock the best of all genres. *These* books,' he pushed Winnie's offering even closer to her, even more disparagingly, 'could have been written by just anyone. They might have been written by a committee . . . of monkeys, or machines. The books I keep here, in the Exchange, they are the kind of books that only one person could have written in each and every case. Each of them is unique. Whichever kind of story they are. You bring me this . . . trash – to replace a novel by Ada Jones? That is an insult, madam. An insult to the integrity of my establishment.'

With that, he turned his back on all of them and hooked

open a door that none of them had noticed before. It revealed a staircase with piles of books on each step. He hurried away, slamming the door behind him.

'Oh dear,' Winnie said. 'I really didn't mean to upset him.' She wrapped up the gaudy romances again and slipped them into her shopping bag. Now she was ashamed of them. 'It's just that . . . I really wanted to keep hold of that book. It meant a lot to me . . .'

The Goth girl slid off her stool and came towards them. To Simon's surprise she suddenly gave them a beaming smile. She didn't seem half as fierce.

'Oh, don't mind him,' she said, taking their membership cards off them and examining the books they had returned. 'Terrance is often like this. Up one minute, down the next. And you really hit a nerve. Offering to swap those terrible schlocky books for one of his. It was a *bit* of an insult.'

'It wasn't meant to be.'

The Goth girl shrugged carelessly, making her silver bracelets and earrings (spiders! Simon realised) tinkle and shiver musically.

'You don't absolutely *have* to return everything you take from here,' she said. 'You can keep them to yourself for ever if you want. After all, you've bought them from him. But,' and here she looked at them warningly, blinking through thick, sticky black mascara, 'you must realise how protective Terrance is, of his Exchange and all the books in it. They have all been chosen by him and they are all important to him. It's just that . . . when they find a good home with someone . . . he gets a little touchy. That's all.'

The girl gave them back their membership cards, having carefully written in Biro what credit they would receive. 'Maybe you think he's peculiar,' she said. 'Minding about his books so much.'

'No,' said Simon.

'Not at all,' added Winnie.

'This place, and his books,' the girl said. 'That's all he's got, really. We are the only real people he ever sees.' She smiled at them – wryly and lopsidedly – as if to say: 'Amazing, isn't it! We're his only real people! And how real are we, eh? How real do *you* feel?'

The way she talked made Simon feel included in something. It wasn't a feeling he was used to.

'Will you have coffee?' the Goth girl was asking now, going over to her gleaming, futuristic coffee machine. She was clearly trying to make amends for the awful way her employer had spoken. Temperamental – that's what he was, thought Simon. He was disappointed in him. He'd seemed so nice last week. Maybe it was his condition that made him fly off the handle like that? He tried to think back – to whether he'd ever known any other amputees – in books, or in real life. Had they been temperamental too?

Simon wandered into the stacks, aware that the girl was being nice to Winnie and presenting her with one of those very tiny cups and saucers. Simon could smell the strength of the coffee in the steam.

'I'll take your son one, too . . .' he heard the girl say.

'Son?' Winnie laughed, flattered. 'Simon's my grandson.'

The girl set the coffee machine juddering and rumbling again. She held another miniature cup under the gleaming spout. 'You have the same address. Do you live with his family?'

They're talking like I'm not even here, Simon thought. He strained to listen without turning as his gran lowered her voice.

'Simon . . . um, lives with us. Myself and his grandad. For the past few months or so.' She sounded self-conscious at answering this girl's questions so freely. 'His parents passed away, you see, earlier this year.' She dropped her voice still further. 'It was a terrible accident.'

'I'm sorry,' said the Goth girl.

Why do we always have to get into this? Simon thought

furiously. It was the first thing any new people would ever know about him. His parents have been killed tragically. He's having a hard time. Be careful with him.

Then that nosey Goth girl was standing at his side. She'd crept up on him as he was staring into space.

'What's this?' Simon looked at the tiny cup. 'Is this for me?'

The Goth girl tutted. 'Of course it is. I didn't know how you have it, but I figured bitter and black.' She looked him up and down.

Simon blushed. 'Really? What made you think that?' He felt absurdly flattered, but didn't know why. Bitter and black. It sounded cool. Like a vampire or a hardbitten detective. Really, though, Simon liked his coffee with frothy milk, two sugars and a jaffa cake or two.

'I'm Kelly,' the girl said. 'You're Simon, aren't you? I've just been having a talk with your grandmother. She seems like a very nice lady to me. I think Terrance has upset her, talking like he did. He can be awful. I've seen him chuck people out of here. I've seen him grab hold of them and just about duff them up for having no taste, or being too noisy, or not respecting the Exchange.'

Simon's eyebrows shot up. 'But – how could he grab hold of people when . . .' Then he stopped dead. It was probably rude to draw attention to the poor man's affliction and his artificial arms.

'Ah,' said Kelly, and took a sip of her own coffee. 'When I say he grabbed hold of them and threw them out . . . I didn't mean it literally, of course . . .' She pulled a face. She'd been caught out exaggerating. Lying, almost, and she didn't really care. Simon liked that. It was as if, to her, the story was the main thing – not the actuality. 'Really though, Terrance is a demon when he's angry. And he's so protective of this place. I'm surprised he ever lets anyone take any books away.'

'Well, I'm glad he does,' Simon said. 'I think it's brilliant here. It's amazing. There's books here you'd never find any-where else. Things I've never even heard of . . .'

'You've noticed that, have you?' She turned to run her hands speculatively across a row of outsized hardbacks. 'Lost books, old books, unique books. Books out-of-print, and some never-in-print. Forgotten books and remembered books. Banned books and books disowned by their authors. There's nowhere else like this. Nowhere else in the world, I bet.'

'I can believe it,' Simon breathed. The two of them were staring at each other.

'What have you found today?' She spoke more jauntily,

lightening the mood. The two of them had become a bit intense.

'One or two things . . .' He shrugged. He wasn't used to talking about his reading. This realisation came as a shock to him. He and Winnie went shopping together and they read for long hours in the same living room, but they hardly ever talked about the books themselves. And there was certainly no one of his own age that Simon ever talked about fiction with. Any other kids he'd known would have recoiled from spending so much time trying to make all those tiny, inert words mean something worthwhile. To them it seemed like too much effort. They just didn't see it. He got some strange looks when he was in his favourite place at the back of the school sports hall, reading. And when packs of kids went by they would look at him like he was crazy.

He couldn't go anywhere without the security of at least two novels in the bag he carried everywhere. (Two, in case he finished the first. He needed to make sure he had *enough* to read. What if he got trapped somewhere? In a lift, or at the very top of a building, and had to wait hours and hours to be rescued?) To him, having these hundreds of pages, these millions of words, forever about his person, meant that he could escape into his own pocket dimension at any moment he liked. He could have another voice talking to him in calm, measured tones. A voice that had nothing to do with his real life. A voice taking him away from the panic of the current moment.

That was exactly how he felt about his life. The panic of the current moment. Dead right. He needed to feel ready to bolt and flee. He was claustrophobic, or was it agoraphobic? Too hot, too cold. And that's how he felt right now. With this strange girl's dramatically made-up eyes staring straight into his.

'I like you,' she said.

'You what?' He answered bluntly, shocked by her directness. He thought she was mocking him. He sounded rude.

'I do,' she said, unfazed. 'I like the look of you. You've been through a lot. You're interesting. Not just some kid.'

He frowned. 'What do you mean, "been through a lot"?'

'It's all right,' she said. 'You don't have to explain it all to me. Not right now. But there'll be other chances to talk. If you feel like telling me all about it some day, I'll be happy to listen.'

'Right,' he said. He wasn't sure what to say to this. 'OK. Cheers.'

She sighed. 'You could act a bit more pleased. Here I am,

offering to listen to all your woes and everything. I'm being really considerate here, offering my friendship and time. You could act a bit more gracious.'

What? Simon was too amazed to be offended.

'Just say,' she added, with a shrug. 'If you don't want to be friends, you don't have to be. You look to me like you're not exactly overwhelmed by good friends. But it's your choice, right? And you're really passing up a good thing here, you know. I'm a great friend to have.'

He cut through her gabbling. 'How do you know I'm not exactly overwhelmed by good friends?'

She laughed. 'Saturday afternoon? Out with your granny? Come on, Simon. Who goes out with their old granny on Saturdays?'

He came over all defensive. 'I do! She's good company. She is! Besides, she wouldn't go out at all if I didn't go with her . . .'

Kelly twisted her mouth about sarcastically. 'Yeah, yeah. Anyway, how old are you? You look about fourteen or something.'

'I'm sixteen!'

'Thought so. You're a bit young for your age. Not exactly babyish, but not fully formed yet.'

'Fully formed!' he burst out. He didn't know whether she

meant on the inside or the outside and suddenly he didn't really want to know. She was rude and awful.

But he wasn't about to tell her that. He didn't want her to stop talking and go. Even though just about everything she said was annoying, he didn't want her to stop.

'I'm a year older than you,' she said. 'I'm an older woman.'

'So?' He smirked. He could be just as cool and sardonic as she could. Just some girl.

'You should make use of my greater experience and knowledge of the world. You should value my superior maturity.'

'Really?' he said.

'Definitely,' she shot back. 'I've lived more than you. I've seen more and done more, and I've read more books, too.'

Now this last bit stung. The rest he didn't care about. That just sounded like the usual teenage showing off, just like the kids at school: bragging about what they'd done. All the sex and drugs and extreme sports and all that rubbish. But no one had ever challenged him on reading novels. It had always been assumed and understood, amongst everyone he had ever known: Simon had read more than anyone his own age. He'd read more than almost everyone.

Now here was this Kelly, looking so smug.

'It's true,' she said. 'I read all the time. I read loads.'

'Novels?' he asked. He was irked.

'Nothing else,' she said. 'I hate non-fiction. Loathe it. It makes me feel like I'm meant to be memorising facts. Fascinating facts! It feels too much like schoolwork, and learning things by rote.'

'I hate non-fiction, too,' he said. 'Except biographies. I love those.'

'Oh, of course, biographies,' she said. 'I should have said they were OK. Great big fat ones, full of terrible scandal and gossip and fabulous photos. My favourite ones are of painters and writers.'

He nodded. 'God, yes. And film stars. I like reading about where they lived and who they knew and who they fell in love with . . .'

Kelly locked eyes with him at just that moment. 'Oh, really?' she grinned. She bit her bottom lip, smearing her purple lipstick. 'All those books are about love, aren't they? All the novels. Anything decent you read. That's all they're about, really. Aren't they? Love?'

He looked at the floor – at the faded, swirling pattern of the carpet. 'I suppose so,' he said. 'I've never really thought about it.'

She laughed. 'You will. One day soon, you will.'

She was really patronising him now. He shivered with irritation. At least, for a second, he thought it was irritation.

'I'll let you search out for your books,' she said. 'I'll not interrupt you any more. But I've written my phone number on your membership card. I thought I'd spare you the embarrassment of having to ask. What with you being so sensitive and all . . .'

Seconds later, hiding behind the wall in one of the other rooms, he took out his Exchange membership card and saw that she really had written down her number. The cheek of it! That girl really thought a lot of herself. What did she think he was going to do? Just ring her up? One night after school? Suggest that they meet up? Like, on a date or something?

He laughed and shook his head.

Yes. Of course that's what he'd do.

Seven

Ada Jones never had any books of her own.

That family of hers, they never had enough jumpers and socks and coats to go round. Books were their last priority.

It was Winnie who kept Ada in books.

Early on in their friendship they realised that they both loved stories. Ada couldn't read and so Winnie spent the time with her, sitting out in the backyard, spelling the words out in the great big treasury of nursery rhymes and fairy tales that had once belonged to Winnie's mum.

Ada had been grateful, fascinated, then utterly hypnotised by the way her new friend made these rhymes and stories lift off the page. She knew it could be done. She'd a half-formed awareness already that magic like this existed in the world. And then she got a whiff of it – in the opening of that grand book of Winnie's. It was an old, splendid volume with a gold and white cover, its spine and corners frayed with use. The

Children's Golden Annual, it was called, and it was what Winnie used to teach Ada Jones to read. Ada learned fast and greedily. Then she wanted more and more.

They went to the ornate, imposing library in their town. They felt alarmed, just stepping inside. They were dwarfed by the plaster pillars and the vast, translucent dome overhead. They stared at gesticulating lady statues and sombre Latin mottoes, and they attracted hard stares from folk sitting down at the long desks. The people who worked there, flitting purposefully, carrying piles of books, didn't look too pleased to see them either. Winnie and Ada were mesmerised, though, by the tall bookshelves: the endless, faceless order of them.

Where do we even start? they both wondered. Which ones are even storybooks? Where are the books that we would like? The ones we'd be able to read?

They pushed along, finding thick, dull-sounding books. Things that called themselves journals or indexes. Nothing that looked very interesting at all. Nothing at all like the *Children's Golden Annual*. Nothing that, when opened, exuded that particular scent. It was a scent they couldn't quite identify, but one that never failed to promise them tales they had never heard before. Or rather, unheard tales that, somehow, still seemed half-remembered. Or remembered from a dream.

What they both wanted was stories that made them hanker: after other times and other places.

The books in that library didn't seem as if they would do that at all. They hefted them down and opened them up, and inside they found graphs and tables of numbers, everything set out in black and white. They discovered maps which might have been exciting, had they been about adventure and voyages and where monsters dwelled. Instead the maps were about where cabbages were grown or fish were netted.

'What is the point,' asked Ada, 'of books without people in them? Or animals? Or stories or jokes or fights or . . . I don't know. Stuff! All the stuff you ever want in books!'

Winnie tried to shush her. They were still under the echoing stone dome. Ada was forgetting where she was, talking too loud again. She was getting carried away by the thought of books and what ought to be inside them. The disappointment in her voice was stark and obvious, bouncing up and around the cool stone hollow of the chamber. Disappointment at what they had found there.

Moments later, they were thrown out of the place. The librarian grasped them by their shoulders and marched them firmly back to the main doors. Ada was protesting loudly and Winnie's face went beetroot.

So the library wasn't for them.

Instead, Winnie became Ada's library. She was given pocket money by her mum. She was relatively rich and spoiled in a way that Ada wasn't. Winnie could spend her money on books of her own that she could keep for all time. After saving her pennies each week she could afford to buy maybe a book or two every month. She would read them and pass them along to Ada. She even snitched a dab of furniture polish and dusted their shiny covers: that was how she looked after them. Ada was a grateful recipient. She was grateful, but not really very gracious. She was demanding.

Ada had soon learned to read much faster than Winnie, and demand outstripped supply. So she wound up reading these books again and again. She could memorise them and embellish them with touches of her own: these tales of genii, pirates, fairies, princesses, serving girls, phoenixes and dragons. She learned what made them tick and she learned to take them to pieces and put them back together. And so, without telling anyone – not even Winnie at first – Ada started to make up her own stories. To herself, inside her mind. Never writing anything down in those early days, just retelling the tales to herself like mantras and imagining them in plush detail as she lay in her shared bed. She was cramped into the hot, sweaty bed with three of her siblings, under the damp eaves of their attic. Mam and Dad's good winter over-coats were heaped onto the blankets for extra warmth and, in that giddy, feverish heat, Ada's stories bred like germs. Changing the tales slightly each time, she told and retold them to herself, and she found that her supply of tales was inexhaustible. They became more elaborate. They became more her own.

The night that she realised this, Ada Jones sat up straight in the crowded bed and, to the muffled complaints of her brothers and sisters, started laughing. She was trembling, full of glorious awareness of what she would do for the rest of her life. By then she was just over ten years old, and she knew. She knew with complete certainty that if she could just keep the story she had only just invented inside her head till morning – if she could keep on remembering all its twists and turns until the dawn broke and she got up and went to find a pencil and paper from somewhere – if she could just do all that, then she would have started off on a course that would occupy her for the rest of her life.

'She was ten and she simply knew,' said Winnie. 'I was the one who answered the door to her. She came banging on ours at the crack of dawn the next morning. I thought there'd been some disaster. But she was wanting paper and pencils. They had nothing she could use round their house.'

Simon was impressed by his gran's tale. 'You're the one who started her off then, really. Giving her her first lessons . . .'

His gran smiled self-deprecatingly. 'Oh, I just happened to have a little writing book lying around. I'd been given it at Christmas. I'd not even started writing anything in it. I was keeping it . . . for something special and worthwhile. I don't know what.' She paused, turned back to the cooker, giving all the pans a quick, perfunctory stir. She was stewing beef in Guinness and thyme for a pie and the kitchen was filled with delicious scents. 'Maybe,' she went on reflectively, 'that's the difference. Ada knew she was a writer, a born writer, at the age of ten and it was just dead natural to her, to take that book off me when I offered it. To take it and fill it up with that story she'd been keeping in her head all night. She said it was beating a rhythm in her mind, like a tune. She was humming it – and, when she started to write it down, very messily in my lovely lilac, flowery Christmas book, this first story of hers came just spilling out, for hours and hours. She sat there at our kitchen table, swinging her legs, frowning, scribbling away. Like I say, a natural. It was marvellous to watch, really. Me? I'd kept that book pristine. Like I was keeping it for very best. I'd never have even started it. Let alone filled it up like she did. I'd have worried too much about spoiling it – this lovely book – with the kind of rubbish that I'd write.' Winnie laughed sadly and came back to sit with Simon at the table. She had set him on to whittling the stalks and outer leaves off the Brussels sprouts. 'Does that sound daft?'

'I know what you mean,' said Simon. He had a whole collection of beautiful notebooks himself. He loved stationery. But he hardly ever used it. Like his gran, he felt that he'd be spoiling it, even trying to put his thoughts and ideas onto paper. He'd tried a couple of times, but became too embarrassed and self-conscious in the attempt. By now he knew that he'd never be a writer. 'We're readers. That's what we are,' he told his gran. 'And we read enough to know that we can't do it. To know that writing is hard.'

She was examining his handiwork with the sprouts. Hm. He wasn't too hot with vegetables, either.

'Making difficult things look easy,' Winnie said suddenly. 'That's what I like. Like Fred Astaire dancing, or Ella Fitzgerald when she sang Cole Porter. Or . . . Vincent Van Gogh when he's gone splashing and swirling colours everywhere. He just loved all that thick, colourful paint and it came natural to him. That's what Ada had – and still has. She had it the very moment she started writing. She made it look easy. She made it sound natural. Well – I was ten as well. I knew I could never do that. Of course I'd wanted to have a go. I loved my books. I was determined then to write my own. But nothing would come. Nothing that would ever be as good as Ada could do. So she put me off, you see, really. I had to be content to be just a reader.'

'There's no "just" about it,' said Simon. 'That's what we are. Proper readers.'

Winnie glanced at him – a sly look. An appraising look. 'That nice Kelly in the Exchange. The Gothic girl. She seems like a proper reader too, don't you think? Hm?' Winnie watched for his reaction. 'Don't you think so, Simon?'

Of course he did.

He didn't want to. He wanted to think that Kelly was silly or boring or easily dismissible from his mind. But she wasn't any of those things. She was brilliant and difficult and sparky and could be nasty and sharp-tongued sometimes and yes, she had read more than Simon had.

And she scared him.

Not in the way that the kids at school did, or the ones who hung about the phone box in the town square. He didn't mean that kind of scary. She was a Goth, all right: all decadent and monochrome and vampy as hell, but it wasn't Hallowe'en type scares he meant, either.

The thing was, he wasn't sure how or why Kelly scared him. Unsettled, maybe, was a better way of putting it. Her gaze was too fierce and probing. She stood too close. She asked him things too directly and he was never sure what she was thinking. He was starting to suspect that she tried to sound sexy and seductive when she talked to him – especially on the phone – and that scared him too.

He had phoned her twice since last Saturday. They hadn't actually talked about much. That had been Simon's fault. He knew he was useless on the phone. He hardly ever used it and tended to clam up, becoming monosyllabic, when he did. In his grandparents' bungalow the phone was in the tiny passageway between the bedrooms and the living room and all the doors were ajar. The first time he called Kelly, he was acutely aware of his gran and grandad in their easy chairs in the next room – frozen, ears pricked, listening in as Simon talked to this girl.

Kelly played it very cool. Between his terror and her cool, the first call didn't get very far. Simon asked if she would be at the Exchange next Saturday. She would, she said. She was there every Saturday. After that Simon panicked, realising he didn't know much else about her life. He didn't even know who she lived with – her parents? Did she have parents or brothers or sisters? He couldn't very well go asking that now.

It would sound too awkward and fake. Instead – and he didn't know where this came from – he asked her if she would like to come and visit his town, one night after school.

'Your town?' she said, still being cool. 'Your town's a dump.'

'It's all right,' he said – getting defensive over a place *he* thought was a dump, too.

'I might come,' she said. 'Wednesday? I've got nothing better on.'

'You could have tea round here. Meet my grandparents properly.' Simon could have kicked himself. I'm offering her a really wild time, he thought. I bet she can hardly contain herself at the thought of it.

'OK,' she said. 'Sounds all right.'

He couldn't believe it. Was she being sarcastic? Would she stand him up, just to make a fool of him, to pay him back? Maybe it should be the other way around. Maybe he should be offering to get on the bus to go to her town on Wednesday after school. He should do the gentlemanly thing and do the travelling himself and pay a visit on her, instead. But she hadn't invited him and besides, the idea of travelling all that way on the bus at night made him shiver. Kelly sounded like she didn't mind. Anyway, what would they do at hers? What did people – teenagers – *do*, anyway? Hang around phone boxes? Slug back cider? He didn't know. At least here they could have a proper tea. He tutted. I'm inviting her to some Jane Austen thing, just about.

'Hang on,' he said. 'I'd better clear it with my gran. I'll ring back tomorrow night and let you know. Plans. Times. Arrangements.'

'OK,' Kelly said – still sounding cool. But there was something else in her voice. It couldn't be excitement, surely. Probably she was just about to laugh at him.

After he had rung off – their goodbyes were just as awkward as the rest of the conversation – Simon returned to the living room. He was about to pick up his book and get on with it, when he realised he had both grandparents' beady eyes on him.

'Did we hear right, Simon?' asked Winnie. Her eyes were shining with mischief.

'We weren't listening in,' said his grandad gruffly. 'Well, maybe your gran was. You know what she's like. She made me listen.'

Simon sat down and smiled like he didn't know what they were on about. 'We didn't talk about much,' he said. Then, immediately, he felt himself colouring. 'Anyway, she's just a friend.'

His gran started to fan herself with her novel – which was

another early Ada Jones she had never read before. 'Do you know what I think, Ray?'

'What's that?' said the old man, cracking into a rare grin.

'I think our Simon has found himself a girlfriend.'

'Don't be daft.' Simon frowned. 'It's not like that.'

'That's what you say now,' Grandad said. 'That's how these things start off.'

'Wednesday, then?' asked Winnie. 'That's when we're going to meet her properly, is it?'

'You've already met her,' Simon said. 'It's Kelly from the Exchange.'

'The Exchange?' said Grandad, baffled.

'Oh, but it's different, meeting her like this,' Gran said. 'Here, at home, having a nice tea. She's a lovely girl, Ray. You might be alarmed at first. By the way she dresses and makes herself up . . .'

'Why? What's the matter with her?' He darted a suspicious glance at Simon.

'She's one of these Gothics . . .' Winnie told him.

'One of these what?'

Gran shrugged, waving her book about. 'I don't know. It's hard to explain. She looks like she's going to a funeral, or something.'

'What? Why?'

'I don't know. It's just the style. Loads of the kids do it.'

Grandad Ray looked completely lost. 'Simon doesn't. He dresses quite normal.'

I do, thought Simon. So normal it's boring and weird. Don't all Goths flock together? Why would someone like Kelly want to hang around with me? Then another thought struck him. Maybe she'd want him to go Gothic as well. Surely not.

'So . . .' Gran said, smiling broadly, and still a little mischievously. 'You'll want some fancy cakes and sandwiches for Wednesday, won't you? And all the best china out . . .?'

Simon shrugged. 'I'm sure she won't expect anything special . . .'

And as soon as he said this, he knew it was wrong.

That was something very particular to Kelly. And it was one of the reasons she unnerved and even scared him.

Because she looked *exactly* as if she was expecting something special, all the time.

Much later that evening Gran was boiling up a pan of milk for Grandad's cocoa. Simon was despatched to the den in the garage to fetch him.

'I don't know why he always wants to be in that gloomy, draughty place,' Winnie said.

'I think he's fed up with us reading every night,' said Simon, looking as she watched the milk foaming and frothing, almost to the lip of the pan. 'He said something about it the other night.'

'He did, did he?' Winnie gave a harsh little laugh. 'Listen, the day he stops making us watch all his horrible news programmes and his rotten football, and when he stops playing his *Themes from the Westerns* records, then I'll stop my reading and he can have my undivided attention.'

Her tone sounded unusually sharp to Simon. He took the tray with the mug of cocoa and plate of ginger snaps and went off to see Grandad. As usual, he had to go through his own bedroom to get into the garage.

He nudged the door open without knocking and found Grandad in his battered armchair, completely absorbed in going through a box of magazines and putting them into the correct order. Simon put the tray down on his nest of tables and Grandad was suddenly acting very shiftily.

'Oh, um. Simon. Right. Thanks. That's kind of you.'

Then Simon realised. Grandad was trying to cover the magazines up, so he wouldn't see. He was putting them back into the cardboard box, face down.

'What are they?' he asked his grandad blithely.

'Oh, these,' Ray said, in a tight voice. 'I'm just checking

through my collection. These are from ages ago. They're vintage, really. Antiques. Probably worth something. Your inheritance, these are.' He gave a worried chuckle.

'Let's see,' said Simon, expecting model railways or maritime memorabilia or maybe football programmes.

'Um,' said his grandad, turning over the top few magazines.

'Oh,' said Simon, not touching it. '*Bounce*?' He leaned forward and flicked through the pile. '*Naturists, Ahoy!*? *Glamourpuss*? *Pert*?'

Each cover was technicolour and each showed girls in various states of undress. They seemed like very old-fashioned girls. Simon guessed at the 1950s: they had very red lipstick, hard lacquered hair and those very pointed boobs. Boobs which, in most cases, were only just covered up.

'You've got girlie magazines in here!' Simon gasped. 'So that's what you're doing, all the time in the garage . . .'

Ray flushed with anger. He pulled the magazines back off Simon and put them roughly in the box. 'They're just my collection. They're from years ago. I only got them out to check they're still in good nick.'

Simon was reeling. Just imagine! His old grandad poring over ancient pictures of girls in bikinis. It seemed a bit sad, really, more than depraved. From what Simon had seen, the pictures were pretty tame stuff. Mildly titillating, compared with what went on these days. They came from a more innocent age. But still his grandad was flustered and cross at being found hoarding them.

'You won't tell your gran I've got them, will you? She needn't know.'

'Of course . . .' said Simon.

'I told her I'd chucked them out years ago. She wouldn't even have them in the house. She thought they were disgusting. Well, you've seen. They're harmless. Just glamour things, really. But I've got to hide them in here, up in the rafters of the garage. Here, give your old grandad a hand, would you? Getting them back up in their hidey-hole . . .'

'Sure,' said Simon. He had to stand on the armchair to get the box back up in the rafters. He wasn't sure that his grandad ought to be clambering around like this. Not at his age.

'Unless you want to take a look at them?' his grandad said.

'What?'

'Well,' said Ray, trying to give a blokey laugh and nudging him in the side. 'You're a growing lad. It sounds like you've got yourself a little girlfriend. It's only natural, after all, for you to be taking such an interest in the fairer sex.'

'Right,' said Simon. He wished Grandad would shut up. This was embarrassing.

'There's some beautiful girls in these magazines,' said Ray. 'Still, I bet none of them are a patch on your – what's she called? Kelly? Aye – I bet you've got an eye for the ladies. Like your old grandad, eh? I bet you take just after me.'

Simon pushed the box back into its hiding place, up between the rafters. Then he hopped back down from the armchair. 'You'd better drink your cocoa,' he said. 'It'll get a nasty skin on it.'

'Ah,' smiled his grandad. 'I've embarrassed you, haven't I? All I wanted to say, son . . . is how glad I am. That you're knocking about with this young lady. That you're starting to do . . . normal things for a lad of your age. That's really good, after all your trauma . . . and the tragedy and all that. You'll soon see – that life goes on. And I was worrying about you, you know. The way you were filling your head with books and nothing else. I was worrying that you'd turn out funny. But that was wrong, wasn't it? You've gone and got yourself a proper girlfriend.' Grandad was grinning at him, warming his purple fingers round his mug. 'And that makes me proper proud of you, son. You're a good kid. You're a credit to your gran and me.'

Eight

Most of the trees were bare now, their leaves turned into this sludgy paste all over the pavements, starting to frost over as the street lights went on. Simon headed out to the super-market with a list of things they needed for tea that night. His gran had written down things like sponge fingers and fancy little cakes and a tin of red salmon. Proper party food. She was probably going too far. Making too much of an effort. Simon was touched by it, though. It was all for his sake.

He wondered what it would have been like, had Kelly come back to his mum and dad's place for tea. There would-n't have been all this fuss and fanfare. His mum would have been interested to meet Kelly, but she wouldn't have put on a special tea or anything. She'd have backed off a bit and been cool about it all. She'd have known Simon was nervous enough about bringing a girl home.

As he made his way towards the stark white windows of the shop, with their fluorescent money-off posters glaring in the gloom, Simon was trying to picture Kelly – tall, ironic, black-eyed Kelly – meeting his mum and saying hullo. He found that he couldn't. It was like they didn't exist in the same universe. He had a panicky second, when he couldn't picture his mum. He stopped in his tracks, his breath catching in his throat. Had he lost her already? He couldn't see her face when he closed his eyes. Then, suddenly, he could conjure up her favourite coat – a red woollen one with a high collar. Then he could see her long, dark hair and then, lastly, her face. Of course. That was how she had looked. He felt his heart start again.

He stepped up to the supermarket's automatic doors and they swished open, inviting him into the warmth.

He had teatime things to buy. He had to get a move on. There was only an hour till Kelly arrived on the bus and he had to meet her at the stop because, of course, she wouldn't know her way around this pokey little town. Previously, she'd have had no reason to visit here.

He picked up a basket and took out the list his gran had written in her painstakingly clear handwriting.

And he thought: if my mum and dad had lived, and if I was living with them still, forty miles away from here, then perhaps I'd never have met Kelly. None of this would be happening.

He shook the thought away and concentrated on the list. What *was* happening, after all? Nothing out of the ordinary. Nothing special at all.

That night he took the cakes and bread buns and tinned salmon home in carrier bags. There was no way he was using the tartan shopping bag on wheels again.

The leaf mulch was freezing over, turning to black ice, as he hurried along home, ignoring the shouts of the kids at the phone box. Maybe it was all in his head, but their shouts sounded less enthusiastic than they had before. It was as if all the fun had gone out of it for his tormentors. That was because he'd ignored them, he thought. They had never got a rise out of him. Not once. As always, that night he kept his head down, plodding towards home as they howled at him and the sky deepened and darkened overhead. He thought: just south of here, Kelly's getting onto a bus. Especially to come here. She's going out of her way in order to visit me.

In the bungalow's kitchen, his gran was busily washing the whole of her Royal Doulton tea service. Now she was drying each piece of it meticulously. Simon stared warily at the thin china cups and saucers with their delicate pink flowers and their gold trim. Bone china. He hadn't seen these since the funeral. They only came out for the very important occasions.

'Get that tinned salmon opened. Mash it up with vinegar and pepper and little bits of cucumber, and pick out the bits of bone,' Winnie ordered him. 'Did you get the floury baps? Did they have enough left?'

Just then Grandad appeared in the kitchen doorway. He had shaved and his face was gleaming red and shiny smooth. He had smarmed his hair down with Brylcreem and he was in his good dark suit, and reeking of expensive cologne. 'Do I have to wear shoes indoors, Winnie? Would it look strange if I didn't?'

Winnie held up a flustered hand. 'Wear what you want. I haven't got time to sort you out as well.'

Simon thought his grandad seemed disappointed then, that Winnie hadn't turned to examine him; to make sure that he came up to scratch.

This is going to be disastrous, Simon thought, all of a sudden, and with a clear sense of foreboding. It'll be awful. The three of us are being absurd. Like it's royalty coming to see us. Kelly will turn up and see how ridiculous we're being and, even if she doesn't show it, she'll be laughing at us all inside. She'll have to. She's too bright, too ironic, not to.

He set to work on the red salmon finger buns. Well. At least she'll have a laugh and a good feed at our expense.

As it turned out, though – and much to Simon's amazement – teatime went brilliantly.

Kelly arrived bearing gifts. Early Christmas presents, she announced, passing well-wrapped parcels to Simon's grandparents as she stepped into their porch. She called them Mr and Mrs Thompson and shook their hands politely. She had toned down her whole Gothic look, too, Simon noticed. She was still a Goth, but managed to be a tasteful one. You could see her natural complexion now, and her eyes weren't as startlingly zombie-like as usual. Her hair wasn't spiked up. Instead it hung down over one of her customary granny dresses – though today, her clothes just made her look demure and intellectual, rather than terrifyingly eccentric.

Once he had shown her into the bungalow, Simon stood back and watched her operate. He was astonished. She wasn't laconic and teasing and sardonic. She wasn't what he was used to at all. She was charming and modest and she could sip tea out of the best china in the house without a single rattle or tinkle or slurp (which was more than Simon managed).

'You must think we're very old-fashioned and dull,' said Winnie. 'Having tea like this.'

Kelly smiled broadly. 'I love the old rituals,' she said.

Simon almost burst out laughing. Old rituals like pagan dances in the woods! That would be more like it. Smearing herself with leaves and berry juice and worshipping Hecate the goddess in front of a blazing pyre! He stopped himself abruptly. What on earth was he thinking about?

Grandad held out a plate with shortbread on it and, as Kelly took a piece ('Oh! I haven't had this in years!'), Simon watched his grandad glow with pleasure. The old man was wearing a cravat, for God's sake! What was going on?

'This is the first time our Simon has ever brought a girl home to visit his folks,' Grandad said. Why was he trying to sound posh? His voice sounded a bit strangulated.

'Is it?' Kelly turned the full force of her smile on Simon. 'Well – he's a quiet lad, isn't he? He's a good lad. Not one for running around with all the girls.'

'Exactly,' said Grandad, nodding sagely. 'That's how all the trouble starts. Running around too much. No – we always tell him: you take your life at your own pace, son. Don't rush into anything. It's worth waiting for the special one . . . to come along. Don't go throwing your life away.'

'Um, yes,' said Kelly.

'Oh, shush, Ray,' said Winnie, clearly thinking he was speaking out of turn and embarrassing their guest. 'What about your own people, Kelly?' Winnie asked. 'Simon hasn't told us much about them.'

Simon winced. That was because he hadn't even asked. He didn't know anything at all about Kelly's family. To him it didn't really matter. He didn't set the same store as Winnie did, by where and who someone came from. Winnie was obsessed with that stuff. Especially these days. ('Your background is very important,' she'd said to him, only recently – as she'd gone on to describe how Ada Jones had managed to forget her own.)

'I've only got my dad,' Kelly said. 'My mum left us when I was quite little. Dad drives a lorry. He's away quite a lot. Now that I'm older he can go even further. All around Europe. I get a lot of postcards.'

'He leaves you on your own!' cried Winnie.

'We live in a nice block of flats,' Kelly said. 'I've known all the neighbours all my life. It's like a big family.'

'That sounds nice,' said Ray. 'Not like round here. No one talks to you round here. They wouldn't spit on you if you were on fire.'

'Ray! That's not very polite. And anyway, you've got all your old pals down the Legion.'

He rolled his eyes at his wife. 'That's not what I mean. I mean proper community spirit. Where's that round here? That feeling like you live in a real town . . .'

'Here we go,' chuckled Winnie. 'A lecture on the Good Old Days. See, Kelly? You'll be wishing you never came around.'

Kelly shrugged. 'I like to hear about the past. I suppose that's why I read so much. I want to understand what things were like.'

'Oh!' said Ray. 'Another reader.'

'I don't mean history-type things, like battles and wars,' she said. 'I mean, I want to know what life was like for actual people. Like, is it true what all older people seem to say? Was it better in the olden days?'

'Yes,' said Ray.

'Well, I'm not so sure,' Winnie said. 'When you think how poor people were. We had next to nothing, when you think about it. And yet there were some much poorer than us. Ada and her family. They hardly ever had enough to eat.' Winnie sighed. 'Has Simon told you? I've been dwelling morbidly on my early years . . .'

Kelly smiled politely. 'He explained why you were so attached to that Ada Jones novel.' She gave a whistle. 'No wonder you didn't want to give it back to Terrance. You should have told him. He'd have given it to you for free, if he'd known . . .'

'Ah, well,' Winnie said. 'I wouldn't like to go bragging about my famous friends . . .' She let out a silly laugh.

'Who's Terrance?' asked Ray suddenly, feeling left out of the conversation.

'He's my boss,' Kelly said. 'He runs the Great Big Book Exchange, where I work.'

'Oh yes?' said Ray. 'A shop, is it? Is that where these two have been toddling off to, every Saturday?'

'It's not just any old shop,' Simon said. 'It's the most incredible bookshop I've ever been in. It's brilliant.' He grinned at Kelly.

'I'll pass that message along to Terrance,' Kelly laughed. 'It'll do him good to feel appreciated. He's been a bit grumpy, just recently.'

'Have another iced bun, Kelly,' Winnie prompted.

'No, thank you. He sends his apologies, too, Mrs Thompson.'

'Winnie, please.'

'. . . Winnie. He told me to pass on his profuse apologies for being so curt with you last Saturday at the Exchange. He can't think what made him speak like he did to such a valued customer.'

'It doesn't matter,' Winnie said, suddenly very aware of Ray's eyes on her. 'Tell him I don't mind. Everyone has off days.'

'He was awful,' Kelly said. 'Now, if I tell him you kept that book because you were a childhood friend of the author's, he'll more than understand. Anyway, he hopes to see you both again this Saturday afternoon. You and Simon. You're becoming proper regulars.'

Winnie blushed. 'Well, I'm not sure what our plans for Saturday are yet.' She glanced down, and saw that everyone's cup was empty. She picked up the china pot. 'But do tell him that I send my very best wishes.'

As Winnie went off to brew more tea, Grandad was looking piqued. 'The Great Big Book Exchange, eh? So that's where you've both been running off to. I knew there was something. I knew there was some big new attraction.'

Kelly ended up leaving much later than she had planned to. Simon walked out with her to the town square so she could catch the 9.20.

'That was a long teatime,' he said, watching their twin breaths puffing out ahead of them, mixing and crystallising in the dark. 'I'm sorry you couldn't escape sooner.'

'Stop it!' she said. Her old, sardonic tone was returning,

now that they were away from the bungalow and out in the empty street together. 'You don't have to make excuses or sound so bloody gloomy, Simon. I had a very nice time, actually. I really like Ray and Winnie. They were very good to me.'

He shrugged. 'They're OK.'

'You're very lucky. They went to a lot of effort to make me feel welcome.'

'I know,' he said – and he felt like he was whining.

'And they both obviously love you to bits. They've moved their whole lives around to look after you. They should be retired and peaceful and taking care of themselves, and instead, they're looking after a teenager. A big, gal-lumphing, moody teenager.'

'All right! All right!' Simon shouted out. She was laugh-ing now and he pretended to be amused, too, but really he was stung by her words. No one had dared to point out to him how grateful he should be for all Winnie and Ray had done for him. He didn't need it pointing out to him. Not a day went by without him dwelling on it and how he could make it up to them one day, or make it all better, or make them proud of him. Who did Kelly think she was? Weighing in like this, currying favour, buttering them up and then pointing out the bleeding obvious?

For a second, as they strolled along under the harsh sodium lamps he felt a flash of irritation and anger at her.

She had been so pleasant and polite. Everything had come so easily to her. In comparison, he had been rubbish. A jangling bag of useless nerves.

'They really liked your early Christmas presents,' he told her.

She smiled. Her choices had been inspired. An old film theme album for him, and another Ada Jones opus for her. Both dirt cheap from a charity shop, but both extremely well chosen and beautifully, carefully wrapped in paper and ribbons. Simon felt ashamed at envying Kelly her thoughtfulness.

'I'm glad I came all this way to visit you,' she said, as they reached the end of the lane.

What? Was that a tinge of sarcasm in her voice? With Kelly he found it hard to tell. He looked at her and her face leaped out all savage and sharp in the light.

'I – I'm glad you came . . .' he said. 'All that way.'

'You wouldn't have come to my town, to see me,' she said. 'You wouldn't have made the effort, would you?'

'I . . . Well, yes. I would—'

'No, you wouldn't. I've made it easy for you. I took the initiative. I've come all this way and charmed your guardians.'

Guardians? He never thought of them like that. Their legal roles. Like something out of a Victorian novel.

Kelly was glaring at him. 'Why do you suppose I did that?'

He shrugged. 'I don't know. But you really cheered up their Wednesday.'

'What?' she gasped. 'Is that all you've got to say?'

'Um . . .' he stammered. *This* was why he didn't go out with girls. The conversations got this complicated. He was never sure what they wanted to hear, or what he was meant to be saying.

'What about you?' she said. 'Have I cheered you up at all?'

'I don't need cheering up,' he said. He gulped. What had made him say that?

'Yes, you do.'

'Think what you want,' he said.

'I think you're depressed. You need bringing out of yourself.'

'What, like a prawn? A shrimp? Some other miserable crustacean?' Simon's tongue was running ahead of him. They rounded the corner, into the town square. The clock in the centre was at 9.18. Kelly's bus was just about due.

'You're shouting at me,' she gasped.

'No, I'm not. But you're patronising me.'

'I am not!'

'Yes, you are. What are you saying? That you're just the right person to help me "out of myself"? You're just the right girl to help me get over my depression, eh? To winkle me away from my books? To get me over my grief?'

This last phrase surprised even him. He stopped talking then and caught his breath back. Kelly was staring at him.

'I'm going to miss my bus,' she said. 'I'd better say goodnight.'

'Look,' he said. 'I'm sorry if I shouted. It's just . . .'

'It's just the Oldies, assuming that I'm going to be your girlfriend. And assuming I'm going to make everything turn out all right.'

He blinked. 'Well. Yes. That *is* what they're assuming.'

Kelly shrugged. 'They're old. They'll assume what they want to and they'll say what they want to. That's what old people are like. But, you know what? *I'm* not assuming anything, sunshine.'

'Yeah?' He smiled at her. He relaxed a little. Just a little.

'Loosen up a bit,' she told him, leading the way across the road to her bus stop. 'Don't get so uptight. For God's sake don't start making assumptions about *me*, either. I just want us to be mates. I like you, Simon. You're OK.'

He felt like cheering. She was so sensible and straightforward. She was so clear about her feelings. Just then he felt like he would believe anything she said. He felt like he'd do anything she told him to.

'Look! The fat lad's got a girlfriend!'

'Hahahahahaha! Loser!'

'He's got some tall, skinny bird!'

'What does she think she looks like?'

'He's going out with a witch or something!'

At the phone box the kids were falling about laughing. Now they had something new to laugh about.

Simon's heart sank in his chest.

'Who the hell are they?' Kelly hissed, glaring.

'I just ignore them. They're always like this.'

The kids at the phone box were shrieking now. One of them had obviously said something hysterical.

'I'm not standing for this,' Kelly said.

'Your bus!' Simon burst out. 'Your bus is about to turn up. You'll miss it.'

'You're right,' she said.

'Hey, fat lad! Is that your girlfriend? That witchy thing?' The biggest of the lads was bellowing at them, louder than Simon had ever heard. The sight of him walking with Kelly had provoked more noise from the gang than even the tartan shopping bag on wheels.

'Right,' said Kelly suddenly and, before Simon knew what

was happening, she was marching smartly over the road, right up to the ringleader.

'Oooh! The witch is coming over!'

'It's Vampirella!'

'Aaaggghhh! We're so scared!'

Kelly didn't say anything. She judged it not worth her while to engage in witty banter with these kids. Her bus was pulling into the town square. It was 9.22 and she didn't have the time to waste on them.

'What do you want, Vampiros Lesbos?'

'How come you're hanging out with dorky boy?'

Simon started hurrying over as Kelly squared up to the biggest, loudest lad in the group. His face was arrogant and red, with a jutting, stubbled chin.

Kelly didn't say a word.

She punched him in the face.

Quick as a flash she struck out and clobbered him in the jaw. A smart, expert jab that her lorry-driving, rough diamond dad had taught her, many years ago. The loudest, hardest, biggest lad dropped to the ground without a single murmur.

'Bloody hell!'

'She's killed him!'

'She's knocked him out!'

Amen, Simon thought, as he stood frozen on the sparkling Tarmac of the road. Kelly turned on the heel of her Doc Martens and came striding back towards him. She didn't look at all smug. She just looked satisfied. She reached Simon and kissed him lightly and quickly on the cheek.

'Look, my bus is waiting. I'll see you on Saturday with your gran at the Exchange. And thank the Oldies again for my lovely tea.'

Then she was off, skating across the pavement and onto the lit-up bus.

Rather dazedly Simon waved as, seconds later, the double-decker went shunting and snorting past him, Kelly its only occupant, waving back.

Now he was alone in the town square, with the kids at the phone box clustered around their fallen leader.

'Do something!'

'Phone for an ambulance!' one yelled.

'We can't! The phone's knacked!'

Simon turned to hurry away. He didn't want them coming after him. He kept on walking and didn't look back, as the kids at the phone box panicked and gibbered.

They had forgotten all about him. For once he didn't have their insults ringing in his ears.

Simon went home ringing instead with triumph and admiration. He could hardly wait to get back and tell his gran and grandad what Kelly had gone and done.

He was so keen to get back quickly that he missed his footing and slipped hard on the fresh, compacted ice. That hurt quite a lot and he found himself sitting there, on the empty road at the top of their street, flat on his bum, yelling out sharply in pain, and then starting to laugh out loud at everything that had happened that night.

Nine

For a few days Grandad was happy.

'I can overlook all her warpaint and her funny black clothes,' he told Simon. 'I think she's a proper sensible girl. She'll see you right.' There was a spring in his step as he set out for the Legion at opening time.

'It's as if he's the one who's started courting . . .' Winnie said caustically, as she and Simon watched him go. 'He'll be bragging to all his old cronies about how we've got a Gothic in the family.'

Simon tutted. But he was pleased. They had accepted Kelly. The evening had been a great success. Now his life wouldn't seem as limited and closed in as it had before. He had found a friend who was the same age as he was and that gave him some kind of purchase on the world of today.

Grandad didn't even complain when Winnie and Simon came home with a bagful of books from the Exchange that

Saturday. He raised an eyebrow and said, 'You two have been pretty busy. It sounds like an interesting place, this Exchange. Kelly made it sound quite exciting. Much better than just some old shop full of dusty books. Do you think I'd find anything there that I'd like, Winnie? Maybe I should come down one Saturday, eh? What do you think?'

Winnie was frowning and Simon felt odd too, at even the suggestion that Grandad might join them on their Saturday afternoons out. It seemed inconceivable somehow. His grandad was laughing at their expressions then and started asking after Kelly. He looked gratified that she had been asking after him. He glowed and said, 'No, I think it's a very sensible idea, this Book Exchange lark. Giving books back to the shop, once you've done with them. I approve of it completely. We were getting too many of the things in this little bungalow. We needed to give some away, didn't we? When Kelly explained how the Exchange worked, I thought – that's just what we need. We can hardly turn around in this place. We need to give some stuff back. Just to get a little breathing space.'

'Hmmm,' said Winnie, not sounding convinced. 'Anyway, Kelly only helps out there. The Exchange really belongs to a man called Terrance.'

'The Man with Two Plastic Arms,' put in Simon, and

immediately felt silly, because they both turned to look at him.

'Why do you call him that?' asked his grandad.

'Um . . . because it's true. He's got two false arms.'

'How did he lose his arms?' Grandad wanted to know. He had a ghoulish fascination with ailments, mutilations and missing body parts. Simon knew this very well from the war stories and submarine stories his grandad had treated him to, over the years.

'Actually, I don't know,' said Simon.

'It's not the kind of thing you can just ask, is it?' Winnie said primly.

'Kelly will know,' said Grandad. 'Ask her. She'll know the story. She'll have asked him straight out, I bet. There's something very straightforward and honest in her nature, you see. She'll have asked him and found out, because she is interested in her fellow man. She's not held back by fake politeness. She's more like myself in that way, you see. Perhaps that's why the two of us got on so well . . .'

'Oh, you did, did you?' Winnie started laughing. 'Honest? Straightforward? You can't even lie straight in your bed at night. Don't make me laugh!'

Ray started to blush. 'Well, I'm not like you two. You two are more interested in your old books than you are in real people. That's a scandal. It's a wonder you ever talk to any other people at all . . .'

'Oh, shush,' Winnie said, and Simon could see she was growing exasperated with the old man. He was a little tipsy from drinking at the Legion. Today it had turned him playful, which made Winnie defensive, and this could easily escalate into a full-scale row.

'I'll make us a cup of tea,' Simon said.

'She's just what you need,' his grandad Ray piped up. 'That Kelly. She's got both feet in the real world. She says precisely what she means. You know where you are with her. I can't abide a dishonest woman. And . . . she's brave, too. She stood up to them kids who were catcalling you. That takes proper nerve. We could all do with nerves like that. Just to live your life, you need a lot of nerve.'

Winnie tossed her head. '*You've* got a nerve,' she told him fondly.

The following Tuesday Simon dressed for school, as usual, and packed his sandwiches for his lunch hour and put all his textbooks and exercise books in his sports bag with his PE kit, ready for school. He said 'bye to his gran and grandad and set out at eight forty-five, as if everything was normal and like any other Tuesday.

He joined the drift of other kids in school blazers down the hill towards the playing fields and the low, blocky buildings of the comprehensive. He dragged his feet and felt himself growing more surly and withdrawn, putting on his protective school persona like a costume. Finally, he found himself filling up with dread, just as he would on any other Tuesday morning: a day with cross-country, calculus and Chaucer on the cards. In his attempt to seem like nothing-out-of-the-ordinary, he was managing to convince even himself.

When he reached the ominous school gates and the bottle-necking rabble he turned abruptly away from the crowd and darted off down a side street. He hastened along Whickham Way to a particular bus stop. He went quicker, more purposefully. He was self-conscious like he was on CCTV and, all the while, his insides were thrumming with subterfuge. His extremities tingled and he was feeling subversive in every molecule and atom and cell.

He stood at the bus stop alone and he could hear the idiotic chatter and squealing of the kids, two streets away, in the schoolyard. Then the school bells were ringing for nine a.m. and the kerfuffle reached a climax. Then the sudden hush descended as the school day began. The terraced houses all about him seemed to sigh and there he was, tapping his foot at the bus stop.

For the first time in his life, Simon was bunking off.

The sensation was incredible. He felt clear-headed and alive and relieved and like he could suddenly go anywhere or do anything. Now he could see how dangerously addictive this was. Never before had he seriously considered truancy as an option. He was a good lad! He was trying to fit in! He was getting his head down and getting through life at his new school. Of course he had never truanted. He had never stepped out of line at all. He'd never even thought about it till Kelly's text arrived in the middle of the previous evening.

I'll meet you on the Express coach. The X50 heading north. We'll go to the city. We can go shopping. We can go running around. Bunk off with me, Simon.

Of course he had to do what she said. There was never any doubt in his mind. This would be just another Tuesday, otherwise. Another dreadful one with narrow-eyed and hostile kids staring at him, and his getting tangled up in equations that had to be integrated or differentiated, and his plodding along behind everyone else through soupy black mud, breathing raggedly and heavily, tasting blood at the back of his throat.

No, here was a chance to make this Tuesday unique.

He'd been too soft before, too obedient. Now he had a friend. It was worth taking a risk to spend a day together. Something as mundane as waiting for a bus seemed thrilling now. There was a glamour to it. A point.

Here it was now. Bound for the north and the big city. Passing through the small town, trundling down the sharp decline to the stop on Whickham Way. And here was Kelly sitting at the back, with her hands and face pressed up to the glass, banging on it to get his attention. Today she was in full, devastatingly Gothic mode. She was like a lady vamp from a 1930s Universal movie, Simon thought. And he was proud to be getting on this coach, paying his fare and hurrying down the aisle to sit beside her on the back seat. She was his companion for the day. His shopping buddy; his accomplice; his partner in crime. She was wearing spikes around her throat and her wrists, and her hair was just about standing on end.

'You did it!' she laughed, as the bus pulled away. 'You're skiving off! You're actually doing it!'

'Of course,' he said. 'I said I would, didn't I?'

'I thought you'd back out. I thought you'd be a good boy in the end.'

He scowled. Only because she was almost right. Over breakfast, stirring sugar into his porridge, watching his gran fold his green polyester football shirt, he'd come close to losing his nerve and backing out.

Now the bus was surging forward, swinging round the roundabout at the bottom edge of the town. It shot into freedom and country roads and yellow, fallow fields stretching miles all around. And here, suddenly, it met the larger roundabout and the motorway. All four lanes, north and south, were chock-a-block and sizzling. Within minutes they had left his town for dust.

'It's easy to forget how close we live to the motorway,' he said. 'All these people, going places. When you're here, zooming along, you needn't even know our town exists. . .' He looked round at Kelly, who was busily backcombing her hair even more. 'Do you bunk off much?'

'Only when I have to,' she said. 'Enough to keep me sane. No one is any the wiser, though. Dad doesn't care. So long as I keep up with my studies.'

'Is he abroad now?'

She nodded. 'He just wants me to get all my exams. But he wants me to have a life, as well. And that's what we're doing, aren't we? We're going to have a life.'

Simon grinned. Inside him though, he felt a bit squeamish and tight with worry. It wasn't often that he went up to the city. Winnie found it too oppressive and harried, especially in these weeks running up to Christmas. The people there carried on daft, she said. People were pushy and they forgot all their manners. That took all the fun out of it for her. So she and Simon had spent most of their Saturdays in smaller towns.

Also, he knew, Winnie wasn't keen on going back to that city on the coast. It was where she had grown up: where the docks and shipyards and back-to-back houses had been. She didn't want to be going back too often. It was changing too much. It was all very different. They were improving it, really. But the city was no longer her own and that unnerved her. She would get flustered and lost in the place that held all her earliest memories.

But now Simon was going there with Kelly, instead. In some small, strange way, it felt almost as if he was betraying his gran. Travelling without her. Shopping and seeing the sights and the people without her. Spending a day out with someone else. Simon experienced a small pang of conscience. Yet that probably had as much to do with panic and the squashing of everyday dread as anything else.

The further north they went, the craggier and hillier the landscape became. The motorway cut through clefts of pale sandstone and drew nearer to the coast so that, every now and then, they would glimpse a silver gleaming sash of sea running alongside them. Simon wondered if it would be rude to read his book during their hour's journey, and decided that Kelly wouldn't mind. She was, meanwhile, staring abstractedly at the windswept coastline and the heavy, almost purple, Novemberish clouds.

Simon wondered where she would want to go. He had never shopped with a girl his own age. Would he have to hang around while she messed about with shoes and bras and nails and make-up? Would she want to go to weirdo shops that reeked of incense, or tattoo parlours where the air was rank with blood and ink? And would she convince him to have a tattoo done or have some part of his anatomy agonisingly pierced?

He'd buy her lunch, he decided. It would be his treat. They'd go somewhere not too expensive, not too tacky, and they'd eat duck and hoisin sauce, or fajitas with loads of sour cream and avocado and fiery hot salsa. He wanted to say thank you, for bringing him out.

He looked at his watch as the motorway petered out and they pulled into the suburbs, past jumbo-sized supermarkets and car parks, and looming tower blocks and breweries with funnels belching tangy smoke. By now, he thought, at school, he'd be finishing the morning's bracing cross-country run. He'd be coming in last, lathered in black mud, trudging heavily towards the showers. Kelly had saved him from all of that. She had given him something to look forward to, instead. It's so easy just to walk away, he thought. To do something great instead.

Then they were crossing the high, broad bridge over the river, and zooming through dark underpasses, and at last they were pulling into the bus station.

As they disembarked Kelly said, 'It's dead rough round here. Keep your hand on your wallet.'

It was so like something his gran might have said, Simon almost laughed. Looking at the deadbeats hanging around the station, though, Simon didn't feel worried. Kelly was the hardest-looking person in sight.

He went to the nearest cashpoint and took out a cool fifty quid.

Kelly whistled. 'You're loaded,' she said.

'I want to buy us lunch.'

'Big spender.'

'Insurance money,' he mumbled.

'What?'

He explained how he'd come in for a bit of money when his parents died. 'I'm suppposed to save it all for when I go to college. It's my nest egg, Winnie always says.'

'Right,' said Kelly. She led the way up the street towards

the city centre. They marched quickly past the cheap shops; the everything-costs-a-pound shops and the amusement arcades. Simon had never seen so many charity shops in one place. Somehow the volume of them was depressing, and it robbed him of the desire to go into any of them.

'It's no consolation, is it?' Kelly said. 'That bit of cash. In exchange for your mum and dad. Any amount of money wouldn't have been a fair exchange.'

'Of course not,' he said quietly. Straightforward and honest, Grandad had described her. Forthright. Sometimes, though, that could come across as tactless.

'I don't remember my mum much,' Kelly said. 'I never really knew her.' She was thinking hard, squinching up her painted eyes, shaking her spiky head. 'But if anything ever happened to my dad . . .' She clicked her tongue and whistled. 'I can't even imagine it. Doesn't bear thinking about.'

Simon found he was touched by this. 'Doesn't he mind?' he asked. 'About the way you dress and everything?'

'Ha,' she said. 'You should see the pictures of him when he was our age. Unbelievable. He shouldn't have been allowed out, really. He was shocking.'

They walked for miles that day, looping great distances around the city centre, popping into record stores and bookshops as and when they pleased. They walked down to the riverside and under the old, dripping arches to visit smaller, more esoteric shops. Simon stood patiently in a hippy shop called Guru as Kelly examined earrings and necklaces made from silver, jet and coloured glass baubles. They found a cafe and ate nachos with chilli, sour cream and green jalapeno slices. It seemed very intimate, sharing a large plateful of sloppy food like this. Simon smiled at the careful, birdlike way that Kelly ate. She insisted they have wine at lunchtime, though he wasn't keen. Red wine would give him a headache on the stuffy bus ride home, he knew. But they ordered it anyway, and Kelly looked like she was drinking a goblet of sacrificial blood.

They walked along the redeveloped riverside, glancing up at spruce, new, architectural marvels: spindly pieces of statue; a bouncy footbridge; the spartan, gleaming frontage of a modern art gallery. They tried to imagine what this whole place must have been like when it was docks and shipyards. Back in Winnie and Ada's time.

'Have you ever been round the old streets where your gran grew up?' Kelly asked. 'It can't be far from here.'

'Most of them are gone. Cleared away,' he said. 'I don't know if their houses are still standing. I remember going there once. When I was very young. We went back to visit my great-grandmother in her little house. She was a tiny woman, sitting underneath all these woollen blankets in her back parlour. It was like going back into the past. I remember being quite scared. I must have been a toddler. I was scared they were going to make me stay there, back in the olden days, with this old woman . . .' In telling this to Kelly he found the memory stirring. It was as if the putting of it into words made the pictures and sensations real again. For the first time he thought about how precarious his memory was. Real things could be lost for ever. He would forget. Inevitably, he would forget all kinds of things.

Now they had wandered into these older streets. Where the houses were red-bricked, terraced and seemingly crumbling and tumbling down the hill and ultimately into the sea. They had tiles missing, walls coming down, some had shrubs growing out of their chimney stacks. Everything here seemed derelict and in its final days.

'It must have been somewhere near here,' Simon said. 'I don't remember what the street was called.'

'There's going to be a museum, apparently,' Kelly said. 'I read something about how they're converting an old church. "The Ada Jones Experience", they reckon it's going to be called.'

'Never!' laughed Simon.

'They're going to reconstruct her house inside. Just like it would have been, back in the past, right down to the tiniest detail . . .'

'They should ask my gran,' he said. 'She'll tell them what it was like.' Then, suddenly, he had a very clear image of pale, dirty Ada Jones out in the street here, reaching up to bang on Winnie's mum's front door. Demanding to be let in and to be given paper and pencils and sanctuary. Finding freedom at the kitchen table next door.

Almost every day, Winnie had told him. That's how often Ada had started to come round in order to write her stories down. She would think them up and hone them down as she lay in bed. Then, the next morning, she'd dash round to the kitchen next door, and sit at the table, scribbling away. It was amazing that Winnie's mum – that wizened, wrinkled person Simon himself just about remembered – had put up with such an imposition. Winnie's mum hadn't been known for her forebearance or her patience. She certainly had no love for the mucky family next door. But Winnie's mum – whom the neighbours called the Duchess – liked to be seen to be doing a good turn.

'She was helping this poor, dirty, neglected child with her education. Just by giving her a corner of the kitchen table to work at,' Winnie had laughed. 'I don't know if my mum ever heard that Ada eventually became a writer . . .'

Winnie was the teacher and, for a while, she felt like she was the one in charge.

The smaller, paler, less fortunate girl would sit and gaze steadily as Winnie dispensed her wisdom.

Ada was a quick learner. She drank all the knowledge up. She exhausted Winnie's stocks and supplies and soon Winnie was left standing.

Winnie was still necessary for the actual buying of books, and Ada would take them off her and she would read them aloud to her teacher: whizzing fluently through hundreds of pages. Ada would happily skip the boring bits, or passages she thought Winnie might find too perplexing or difficult. Winnie would sit, stunned, listening to her protégée.

'Chuntering on' is what Winnie's mum, the Duchess, always called the sound of Ada's reading aloud. She would sometimes chase them away from her kitchen table, exasperated at their clutter of papers and books and scratchy pencils. The Duchess didn't see any point in stories. 'There's no profit in reading books. No money in made-up things.' When she delivered a verdict like that, the stout Duchess looked very grand and sure of herself. She was a domineering figure in a stiff white blouse with a black cameo brooch at her throat. As she hovered around her immaculate kitchen, she flicked at stationary objects with her tea towel, as if defying dust to settle. The Duchess liked things to be just so.

She was astonished when Ada answered her back.

Ada slammed her book shut. 'But somebody has to make money out of made-up things. The people who write these books do, don't they?' She rapped scabby knuckles on the hard, shiny cover.

Winnie drew in a breath and took a step backwards.

The Duchess said, 'You cheeky little thing!' She raised her hand, as if to deliver a slap. Instead she flicked out her tea towel, shooing the girls out of her kitchen. 'You've always got a smart answer, Ada Jones.'

'But it's true,' Ada said. 'Somebody has to write these books. They don't just write themselves.'

Winnie wasn't saying anything. She was biting her lip and watching the proceedings and wanting to dash for the toilet outside. She knew her mother was about to fly off the handle at any moment.

'Books,' scoffed the Duchess. 'On a broiling, muggy day like today, the two of you want to sit there with that thing. Filling your heads . . . You should be out getting the fresh, sea air.'

'I'm going to write books,' Ada said mockingly. 'That's what I'm going to do.'

The Duchess sighed at her. 'That was a fine game when you were a little girl. When you were nine and ten and Winnie was learning you your letters and that. When you used to sit here and write your daft little stories. . .' The Duchess's face drooped sadly. She looked anxious now, over how fervent Ada seemed. 'But those games can't go on, can they?'

Ada's body was rigid. 'Daft stories?'

'You've gone twelve years old,' said the Duchess. 'You're nearly grown. You both need to buck your ideas up. You're both far too babyish for your age. You're stuck in your stories with princesses and fairies and fine ladies in grand houses. That's all you care about. But you listen to me. You'll be finishing school before you know it – and then what, hm? The two of you haven't got an idea between you.'

Ada sneered. 'I've got lots of ideas.'

'The wrong ideas,' sighed the Duchess, flicking at the mantelpiece clock with her tea towel. It gave a mournful 'bong'. 'Ideas above your station.' She turned to look at Ada – and at Winnie, too – as she said: 'The likes of us don't write books. Don't be ridiculous, girl. It will never happen. Ever. The sooner you face that fact, the better.'

Winnie watched Ada's face twist for a few moments, as the girl struggled over what to say next. Winnie watched her trying not to weaken and let herself cry. And she managed to stop herself shouting and raving and swearing at Winnie's mum, like she would her own. Instead, Ada's face slowly took on an expression of benign composure. It was like watching blancmange setting. Winnie watched as Ada patiently hid her desires and ambitions out of sight, and faced the Duchess with calm, determined wilfulness. 'I will prove you wrong,' Ada said.

Later, when the sun was going down over the docks, Ada and Winnie sat out in the sand dunes, sulking and plotting. They hid in the long, bleached grass, hunkering down in the sand and slats of golden, eggy sunlight. They gazed through the stripey grass with eyes like feral cats.

'I will, you know,' Ada kept saying. 'I'll prove it to all of them.'

'The seagulls are so loud,' Kelly said. 'They're really screaming. I suppose you wouldn't notice if you lived here all the time.'

They wandered along the seafront, chilled by the breeze that ruffled the water silver. They watched a ferry slide by, in no particular hurry.

'Let's head back into the city,' Simon suggested. This place was beginning to make him feel maudlin. Today was meant to be their fun escape. Here they were dwelling on somebody else's past.

Back in town Simon found himself buying brand new books. In a mammoth chain store, the bright covers and the newness of their smell and their unbroken spines conspired to make him want to own new books for once. He splashed out. He made his choices – novels too recent to be circulating in second-hand shops or the Great Big Book Exchange just yet. He wanted novels without reputations; novels that were so new they were untried, untested. He found the idea of blank, undiscovered territory alluring.

Then he watched Kelly buying black suede boots with money she had been saving since last Christmas, she said. Soon they were walking around with bulging shopping bags, just like everyone else in the city centre. Did that make them feel like they fitted in more? Did they feel that they'd made a few choice purchases, along with everyone else?

Kelly shrugged. 'I've no desire to fit in with everyone else. Not at all. Look at them all. Look at the state of them!'

Simon winced. She'd get into bother if anyone heard her.

Late in the afternoon, the Christmas lights started to sparkle and fizz. They were all animated snowmen doffing hats; holly and mistletoe jiggling about on the municipal tinsel strung between lampposts. Simon and Kelly went to a wine bar, not too far from the bus station. To Simon – used to old ladies' tea rooms and sharing a pot of Earl Grey with his gran – this seemed like the very height of sophistication.

They perched on high stools of stainless steel, at a gleaming glass-topped bar, pretending they were old enough. The waiter brought them bright orange cocktails that Kelly had chosen from a leather-bound drinks list. The drinks tasted potent, sharp, and just a bit nasty. The whole moment was a delicious one and, as they looked out across the city rooftops, Simon couldn't quite believe that this was him. Here he was, out with a girl on a weekday . . . Christmas in the air and they were having exotic drinks, all illegally. This was the high life. This was like novels.

He became quite tipsy. He found he was telling Kelly about how he had discovered his grandad with that stash of vintage magazines.

'Glamour magazines, the old man called them . . .'

Kelly frowned. 'Back in the days when I was a hardline feminist – last year, really – I'd have disapproved of that.

Now I don't think there's much harm in it. And those old mags from the Fifties can be quite kitschy and funny.'

'It was a shock,' Simon said.

'Don't be so prudish.'

'But, you don't like to think of your grandad . . .'

'What? Still having sexual feelings? Hm? What about your gran?'

'Stop it,' he laughed. 'They're both past all that. She's told me that herself. She says she gets all the romance she needs from novels . . .'

Kelly gave a barking laugh. 'Don't we all?' she sighed.

Simon took a large – too large – sip of his odd-tasting drink. 'What gets me, about Grandad and his *Pert* and *Bounce* magazines, and all that, is that they're the only books – the only publications of any kind – that he actually owns. He goes on about me and Gran having all our books and cluttering the place up. And yet all he's got are his glamour magazines. I think it's a bit sad . . .'

'Don't be so snobbish!' said Kelly. 'I didn't think you'd be like that, Simon. Everyone has their own thing, don't they? Their thing's their thing.'

'You what?'

'I said, "Their thing's their thing."'

'Right,' he said. 'That's dead profound, that.'

'You know what I mean. If old pictures of 1950s ladies in the nuddy is what he's into, then that's fine, as far as I'm concerned.'

'When did you change your attitude, then?' he asked. 'Away from the hardline feminist point of view?'

'Oh, when I started working for Terrance, at the Exchange,' she said. 'I could hardly be puritanical about girlie mags there, could I?'

'Why?' he said, not following her at all.

'Because of the little room at the back,' she said, fiddling with the paper umbrella in her glass. 'Ah. You've never found the little room right at the back, have you? Behind the beaded curtain?'

He blushed, suddenly feeling very naïve. 'No. Why – should I?'

She shrugged. 'Probably not. You're too prim. It's where all the old glamour mags are kept. Nothing too shocking, of course. Not really. It's just another line Terrance has going at the Exchange. Ancient, saucy pictures from the olden days.'

He gulped. 'I hope my gran hasn't found that room. She would be horrified.'

'What Terrance has got behind that beaded curtain wouldn't shock anybody, these days. They aren't that rude, compared with today.'

'I think my gran is quite shockable . . .'

'I don't think she is,' Kelly smiled. 'Have you ever read Ada Jones? She can get quite racy.'

'Really?'

'Oh, yes.' Kelly was struck by an idea then. 'You know, I bet Terrance would give your grandad quite a good price, if he wanted to get rid of his mags. If they really are vintage, like you say.'

'I doubt he would want to,' said Simon. 'He had them bundled up like treasure. Hidden in the rafters. There's no way he'd want to get rid. Besides, then Gran would find out what he'd been keeping . . .'

'I suppose so,' said Kelly, slurping up the last of her drink. Simon was finding that he couldn't finish his. 'Aren't people just *weird*?' she said. 'Come on then, sunshine. It's time to get on our bus. Back to the real world for us.'

On the way back south and through the darkness down the motorway, both Simon and Kelly were reading their new novels. They sat in companionable silence aboard the mostly empty bus. It might have been the strong drink and the excitement of a day's escape, but Simon was very conscious of Kelly's proximity, all down his left side. Their legs were almost touching. Her elbow jarred his, each time she turned a page in her book. Simon found himself growing extra sensitive: his scalp tingling; the velveteen of the seat feeling rough through his school shirt.

They reached his home first. Quite abruptly, the bus turned off the motorway and into his town. Their goodbyes had to be hasty.

'Thank you,' he said. 'For today. I've never had a day like—'

She kissed him.

He was standing in the gangway, clutching his bags, leaning down to make himself heard above the wheezing engine noise. Kelly had lurched upwards, in for the kill, and Simon had flinched. He wasn't expecting the suddenness of her moving in, or the warmth and the shocking wetness of her mouth. He found himself flinching and tried to stop himself. He opened his mouth too late, thinking he ought to reciprocate, to be polite and be open to her sudden kiss. But their teeth clashed, hard and painfully, and they both jerked apart.

She laughed. She looked cross and piqued, but she laughed at him, and at their failure. 'Go on, go on,' she said. 'Get off the bus. Or he'll drive off again. You'll be taken away from your town for ever!'

As he hurried off without another word, his heart was

banging away inside him. He felt elated and clumsy and foolish beyond belief.

He jumped off the X50 Express and stood in the roadway
to watch her zoom off.

I messed it all up, he laughed, and I nearly managed to
knock all her teeth out. She probably thinks I'm an idiot
loser and beneath contempt, but . . .! But she wanted to kiss
me. She reached up and wanted to kiss me!

Ten

Simon was careful during the next week. As he quietly went about his business, he was expecting reprisals from every direction. The kids at the phone box would get him, as soon as they saw him alone. They would make him pay for Kelly's attack and their leader's abject humiliation. At school, too, he would surely be made to pay for skiving off. They would definitely find out what he had been up to and he'd get excluded and then expelled.

He was going off the rails. His life was falling apart. His grandparents would be so ashamed of him. He would never go to college now, and he had ruined his life and all of his future hopes. He hadn't even been able to kiss Kelly good-bye properly. He'd cut his lip as they'd parted. He hoped he hadn't damaged hers.

She hadn't phoned since their day out together and, was

it his imagination, or had she been a bit cool with him at the Exchange on Saturday? They hadn't had much time together. For once there had been other customers, besides Simon and his gran, and Kelly had been distracted, welcoming and inducting newcomers to the ways of the Exchange.

She had smiled at Simon and given him a small wave. She took the money for this week's books and stamped his grey membership card, but she didn't talk to him like she usually did. Nobody would have been able to tell they'd shared a day out in the city like they had. Maybe that was the point. Their day together was a secret from Winnie. Kelly didn't want to give that away.

But still Simon fretted. He wanted some sign. He wanted to know that she hadn't gone frosty; she hadn't turned weird on him. But on Saturday there was no chance. And later, he couldn't bring himself to ring her. Their talking last week had been so easy, and natural. He was so stilted when he talked on the phone. If she didn't phone him, then he wouldn't phone her. And besides, he felt too embarrassed, knowing the door to the living room was open; knowing how interested his grandparents were.

As the days of the following week went by, Winnie made a remark or two, about how they hadn't heard much about

Kelly. Had the two of them fallen out? Had the two of them cooled off?

Simon scowled at his gran. Of course they hadn't. There was nothing to cool off about. They were just mates. He tutted and rolled his eyes when his grandad asked after his girlfriend. His grandad had adopted a matey and blokey attitude towards him, nudging and winking as if they shared secrets.

In a way, Simon was dreading seeing Kelly again. She would expect him to kiss her properly next time. That last failure they could blame on the bus, on the way the ground had moved beneath their feet, knocking their heads together. But what about next time? He was bound to do it all wrong again. It wasn't something he had much experience of. He dreaded it. It terrified him. Not because it was her. Anyone would have terrified him, opening their mouths, closing their eyes and glomming onto him like that.

He hated to do things wrong. He was excited and flattered and amazed, yes – out of everyone, *he* was whom she wanted to kiss – but he was more scared than excited, in the end. He knew there was a good chance he was opening himself up to ridicule. That's what happened, when you stepped outside of the things you knew.

That week he returned to his reading with a vengeance.

He had a handful of novels from the Exchange. They were fat, obscure things he had never heard of. The blurbs on their back covers promised labyrinthine plots full of incomprehensible twists. It was a relief to dive into the complexities of these books, and to get to know characters wholly removed from the realm of his own experience. That week he was living with scientists and spies, courtesans, cave men, astronauts, vampires and queens. He read hundreds of pages at each sitting, until his eyes hurt when he glanced from side to side. His eyeballs felt vitrified: as if the pupils were cracked and the irises were crazed with overuse.

Still Simon kept on reading. Even at mealtimes, with the book on the tablecloth, causing his grandparents to comment, but he wouldn't put it away. Bravely, he bunked off school again. When it came round to a full week since his trip to the city with Kelly. As if to commemorate that day his feet were leading him away from the school gates once again. It wasn't even a conscious decision. He simply climbed aboard a bus that took him to Kelly's town.

He didn't visit the Exchange. He knew she wouldn't be there that day. He didn't go looking for her, for the flat where she lived. It would seem like a weird thing to do. Like he was stalking her. He didn't really want to see her in the flesh that day. He wanted to walk around with the *idea* of her. He just liked knowing that he was in the same town as her. He liked knowing that it wasn't completely impossible for them to walk into each other by chance. That was something that could happen. And if it did, then fair enough. He would think up something to say to her. And if he didn't, that was OK too. Probably it would mean that they weren't fated to meet up that day.

He was becoming a great believer in fate.

'You've read too many novels,' Winnie had told him, when they had discussed this subject only recently. 'You're starting to think the whole of life is plotted out like a book.'

'Maybe it is,' he said. 'Maybe it's all written down and fated.' He was thinking about his parents and their accident. Of course, he wouldn't say this to his gran. It would upset her too much. But inside his own mind he was thinking about how his mum and his dad had been killed so quickly, so shockingly.

'I don't think you're right,' said Winnie. 'I think you're thinking too deeply about it. That doesn't do, you know. In my experience, if you think about life too much, you only upset yourself. And that's true. Look at your grandad. He's been in a mood for years.' This had been in the supermarket, with Winnie trying to tear plastic bags off a roll as they picked out fruit. 'I don't believe it's fate, any of it,' she said. 'What kind of story would I be in, eh? What kind of story would that be?'

Simon wasn't sure about that, so he let the matter drop. He had a few ideas though, about what his gran's story might be. It could be a romance, of sorts. Old Terrance, at the Exchange, he'd been looking at her funny. Simon had noticed that much, last Saturday. He was sure it wasn't his imagination.

Winnie had been explaining to Terrance about growing up with Ada Jones, about giving her the Christmas notebook, and sacrificing that treasured object so that Ada could write her first story down. Simon had been listening in, pretending to choose his novels, and he'd looked over to see Terrance's reaction to the tale. The man with two plastic arms looked enchanted. He was staring at Winnie, grinning at everything she said. Simon didn't think that he was just amused by her. There was a glimmer of something else there, too.

Simon noticed another thing. The Exchange owner had smartened himself up. Knowing that Winnie would come, as she always did now, on Saturday afternoon, he seemed to have made an extra special effort with his appearance. His white hair had been washed and tamed so that it lay fluffily close to his scalp. He had shaved somehow, and had managed to iron himself a red chequered shirt. He wore ironed jeans, too. It was as if he was deliberately dressing younger. Trying not to look like a clapped-out old fogey.

Is he really *after* my gran? Simon marvelled, spying on them from between the book stacks.

Winnie was still a handsome woman, Simon thought, trying to look at his gran in an objective light. She was very smart and well groomed. There was something charming and feminine about her, that mature men responded to.

This was amazing! What if they started having an affair? What if they asked him to cover for them? If he was drawn into their lies and deception? He wanted to talk to Kelly about it, but there wasn't a moment in which they could find the privacy.

Definitely, Simon thought. It was definitely true. The way that Terrance looked at Winnie spoke volumes. His eyes crinkling up like that, his mouth twitching at the corners, his nostrils dilating as he listened to her talk about her youth. They were all sure signs. Simon thought about it a lot during the following week. Terrance and his gran were teetering on the edge of grand, reckless passion! A last-minute fling in the twilight years of their lives!

He couldn't bring himself to ask his gran if she'd noticed

anything. But she seemed chirpier after her encounters with Terrance, as if energised by his attentions to her.

But Grandad . . . What about him? What if Simon was caught between his grandparents in some awful tug of love and loyalty?

Simon went over all of this in his mind, on his second day bunking off school. He wandered around charity shops and newsagents and the chilled, damp, indoor markets, relishing the pungent scents of cheese and game and fish. It wasn't often that he walked round these places alone. He went at his own pace: observing, hanging about, mulling things over. He thought about himself and Kelly, and about his gran and the man with two plastic arms. He thought about his grandad at home, sitting in his garage, oblivious to all this life and excitement; all the shenanigans going on around him. His grandad in his den, flipping through pages of bathing beauties in their dayglo bikinis. And eventually, after wandering all day and sitting quietly in cafes, having beans on toast and countless mugs of sugary tea, Simon thought about his mum and dad. And he was shocked that they had been out of his mind so much, and he hadn't even noticed. All of a sudden, they hardly seemed real to him.

They aren't here any more, he thought. Their story isn't

moving onwards through time any more. It's finished and now they can't change. The rest of us are changing every day. We're moving past them and soon they'll be way behind, and out of sight.

He thought about being a little kid and going to see his dad at work. His dad had been a security guard at the small airport not far from their town. From the earliest, Simon had loved to go to see the planes taxiing about; to go behind the scenes with his dad – feeling very helpful and special and privileged. And he thought about his favourite times with his mum: when they were alone and his dad was working lates, they would eat spicy stir-fries and noodles. They would treat themselves to all the exotic food his dad wouldn't eat, and then they would read together, through the long hours of the night.

Simon's parents had been very much in love. He saw that clearly, now that they were gone. The bond between them had been so strong that even Simon had felt a little out of place when the three of them were together. He'd felt like an intruder, almost. Only when he was with his mum or dad alone did they really give their full attention to him.

It had been natural for them to fly off on holiday together, leaving him with his grandparents. They all agreed, he was much more stay-at-home than they were. And he could see that his parents wanted to use this holiday they'd won as a kind of second honeymoon. They wanted to celebrate the life they'd had together, and Simon had waved them off in the departures lounge, at the same airport where his father had worked all their married life. Simon stood with his grandparents at the plate glass windows, waving at the plane as it cruised gently down the runway, even though there was no chance his parents could have seen.

He stopped himself going over these images. He blinked away that last picture of his mum and dad, going off through customs at the airport, his dad's arm round her waist; his mum getting flustered, keeping a hold of all the tickets and documents. He shouldn't dwell on all of this.

Simon focussed on the cafe around him. Another old ladies' cafe. He had been staring at the same page in his novel for the past half-hour. His aching eyes flicked through the same paragraph repeatedly, never taking in the sense of it.

An awful, gloomy sensation of loneliness dropped over him and he realised that he was hopeless at spending his days alone. He shouldn't even have tried. It was too easy to start feeling sad. He thought having a novel with him would be enough to save him. He had thought reading could lift him out of any gloom. Today it couldn't.

He sat in the old ladies' cafe and wished he had company. He wanted to see Kelly.

He wanted to be talking.

Then, as he waited for his bus home, she phoned him.

'Listen, sunshine, are you coming to the Exchange this Saturday?'

His heart was pounding away absurdly. 'Yes,' he burst out. 'Why?'

'I've got some news,' she said. 'I've had an idea.'

'What . . . ?' He couldn't get his words out. All sorts of things were crowding into his head. What did he really want to say to her? I'm in your town? I'm here right now? I'm standing in this queue to go home . . . and why aren't you here?

'I haven't got time to talk now,' she said quickly. 'I'll explain on Saturday. But it's a brilliant idea, Simon. You'll love it.'

'What *is* it?' He was grinning now, carried away by her enthusiasm. 'Give me a clue.'

'OK,' she said, and paused. 'It's about your gran,' she said. 'About something we're going to do for her.'

'For my gran?' He hadn't been expecting that. 'What?'

But Kelly's next few words of goodbye were drowned out

in the rustle and murmuring press of the crowd about him, and the noise of the bus as it arrived at the stop. His phone gave three sharp bleeps as the connection was severed and he knew he would just have to wait till they went back to the Exchange. Kelly would let him know then.

'Things will have to change around here,' said Winnie, dabbing her eyes.

She was so upset she hadn't even asked Simon how his day at school had been. That was good. He wouldn't have to lie. 'What do you mean?' he asked her, coming to sit at the kitchen table. 'What's upset you?'

'Oh, *him*, of course,' she said, trying to smile. 'That silly old fool. It's nothing new. He's just had one of his rotten tempers on him all day long. Ever since he woke up. You know how it is. When he gets worked up like that, it's murder for whoever is around him, and usually that's me.'

'Is he still not sleeping properly?'

'I've told him to get himself down the doctor's surgery and get some tablets if it's such an issue. He claims it's all down to me, though. Leaving the lights on so late, going trekking backwards and forwards and sitting up doing my reading . . .'

Maybe they should have separate bedrooms, Simon

thought. The two of them are out of synch. They'd be happier if they weren't disturbing each other through the night. But they didn't have the space now, to sleep separately and find some peace: not with their orphaned grandson living there. He was forcing them to lie together; to drive each other mad.

'The latest thing he's fixated on is lice,' Winnie gasped, starting to laugh. 'He keeps saying all my books are full of germs and bacteria and lice and all kinds of nasties. He says he can see all these things creeping about through the bedclothes. He can feel them crawling and burrowing through his skin and his hair. All from my old paperbacks that I read in bed. Well, I ask you. That's just silliness, isn't it? He's got himself all worked up over nothing.'

Simon didn't reply. He knew his grandad could get himself into a temper over nothing. He was like a sudden storm blowing up out of nowhere, then expending itself briefly in thunder and hail. Then blue skies would resume and he'd wonder what had caused all the wreckage around him. But Winnie was careless with her husband's feelings, Simon had realised in recent months. She never took any of his complaints seriously. She always continued to do exactly what she wanted to do. She had even grown used, over the years, to disregarding his violent but short-lived bursts of anger.

'It's different these days,' she told Simon. 'He's drinking more at the Legion. I know he is. His tantrums are getting worse. And the way he's talking . . . about feeling infested and claustrophobic . . . it's crazy talk, really, isn't it?'

I'm partly to blame, Simon thought. I'm crowding them out of their home. I'm making it worse for the pair of them. I just make more work for them. I create further tensions.

'You read about old people losing their wits,' said Winnie. 'I'm starting to get worried about him. Yelling at me over the slightest thing. Glaring at me all the time . . .'

'I'm sure it's not as bad as all that.'

Winnie spoke harshly to him: 'How would you know? Your mind's been elsewhere. You've not even noticed how your grandad's been behaving . . .'

Simon blushed. 'I thought he seemed happier. After Kelly came round. He made such an effort. He looked so smart. You said yourself he was cheerful for days afterwards.'

'Well,' said Winnie, getting up to make a start on peeling potatoes for supper. 'That didn't last long. Everything's changed again, with his switch of mood. He was whinging about all of us this morning. I was evil for keeping him awake and bringing too many infested books into the house. You, he reckons, aren't even going to school any more. He says you're skiving off and running about on the buses instead . . .'

Simon's heart started hammering at this.

Winnie continued: 'And now he reckons that your Kelly is just the same as all the other girls. Just a common, spiky-haired tramp, he said. He said she was cheeky, being so familiar, talking to her elders when she came round here. He said she's only knocking about with you because of your insurance money. 'Cause you've got a bit more cash to draw on, more than any other, normal boy of your age . . .' Winnie was reaching into the fridge for the eggs as she said this. She froze suddenly, and looked ashamed. 'I shouldn't have told you all that,' she told Simon.

'It's all right,' he said quietly.

'I'm sure your grandad didn't mean it.'

Simon shrugged. It couldn't be true, could it? Kelly hadn't known he had a bit of cash until they went on their day out together. And besides, it wasn't like he was a millionaire. It wasn't *that* much money. And, anyway, what had his grandad meant: 'any other, *normal* boy' of his age? Did Grandad think he was a freak, too? Like Simon himself did?

His gran was now flustered and cross with herself, for giving too much away. As she set about tremblingly peeling spuds, Simon felt a bit sickened. He felt like he had been eavesdropping on a very private row – and he had heard upsetting mention of himself. His gran shouldn't have said anything, he thought. Now she was standing with her rounded back to him, worrying at the potatoes, letting their dark skins fall away in long, expert ribbons.

Simon spent most of the rest of that evening lying on his bed, keeping out of their way.

His grandad came home in time for supper. He was woozily drunk and quiet, stewing with either repentance or resentment – it was hard to tell which. He dipped hot, glistening chips into the bulging yellow eye of his egg and didn't say a word, to either Winnie or Simon.

Gran was mostly quiet, too. She let out the occasional sigh, trying to draw attention to herself.

Gran's not blameless, Simon found himself thinking, stretched out on his bed, trying to read. I used to think she was perfect. I thought she was kind and all-knowing, full of generosity and compassion and humour and sense. But . . . she's a bit selfish and silly, sometimes. She doesn't know when she's upsetting people. She can't see it. And if she's got something to say, something she has to get off her chest, then she'll just go ahead and say it. No matter who gets hurt as a result.

She steamrollers over people. She would never admit that. She goes on like she's the one who bends over backwards to please and serve everyone else. She would claim that she puts everyone else's needs ahead of her own. And it's true that she cooks and cleans and irons and washes and keeps life here on an even keel (just about . . .). But my gran is a woman who likes things to go all her own way.

Simon suddenly saw his grandad's tempers in a different light. As the thwarted resistance of a man ground down by his wife's dominance.

But that didn't fit either, thought Simon. He thought about the way Grandad Ray talked to Winnie: the way he routinely dismissed and disparaged her. 'Oh, shut up, you daft old woman. What do you know about the way the world works? You don't know anything. You get back in your kitchen. You should stop reading all them novels. They give you ideas. Making you think you know something about the world, about things that really matter. And you don't. You know nothing.'

'He belittles me,' Simon remembered his gran telling him. 'For years and years he's done that. It comes automatic to him. It's a habit. He makes me feel like nothing. Like I'm stupid. Like I'm a bit simple. Like all I can do is cook his meals. That's how he keeps hold of me. Because I end up feeling like there's only him who needs me, or wants me around. I feel like my only purpose is taking care of him . . .'

Now it was late. He wanted to read. He wanted to stop thinking about the lives of everyone around him. Ironically, the book he was reading just then was Ada Jones's first novel, which he was borrowing from his gran. After visiting the old streets by the docks, albeit briefly, last week, he had felt like he wanted to read the novel. He wanted to understand Ada's account of that shared childhood. Simon knew the sights and smells of that place – at least, how they were nowadays. The stiff breeze coming in from the open sea – that must be the same as it was back then. (Just the thought of that sharp chill made his sore lip throb.) Now, he thought, he wanted to hear the voices, too, back in the past.

His gran was on with Ada's fourth novel by now. She was reading them in sequence. Simon lay listening to his gran going to bed, banging the door to the living room, saying a grudging goodnight to Grandad Ray. Simon imagined her sitting up in bed, resolute and stiff, reading her novel, not to be deterred.

Ada's novels seemed to follow the progress of her real, private life. That's what Winnie claimed. Reading deeper and further into the fiction, Winnie was reaching into that unknown life of her friend – following her away from the north, into the south and her adulthood: discovering what had become of Ada Jones.

'And the life she led is so different to mine, Simon,' Winnie had said, sadly. 'Foreign travel. The best restaurants. Famous people. She must have been everywhere. She's got all the culture and knowledge and class. It's all very glamorous. A million miles from where she started out. And all the men, too! All the husbands and . . . lovers. She's had a wild life, really, if even half the things in her books are true. Ada's had a rare old time of it. Really, I've done nothing – nothing! – with my life, compared to her . . .'

Ada's reading should have put her streets ahead at school. Winnie knew how good she was but the teachers never did.

Their school was high-walled and red-bricked: the rusty colour of dried blood, Ada always said. It was on a hill over-looking the docks, surrounded by sandy dunes and tussocky grass. It was a high, bleak place, fenced in and prison-like: the teachers flapped around in black robes like rooks.

All the teachers thought Ada a waste of their precious time. She showed no interest, nor any special aptitudes. She was one of the slow-witted mass that swelled the dark corridors and filled the assembly hall: all of them destined for, at best, lowly jobs in the factories or the dockyards. Most of the girls would stay at home. They would turn themselves into facsimiles of their mothers, tending to children and men; scrubbing doorsteps, nappies, pots and pans.

Winnie watched Ada at school. She marvelled at the girl's quietness and smallness; her way of blending in. Ada sat at one of the desks at the back. Even at thirteen, fourteen, her legs were too short to reach the ground. She cast wary glances about, keeping her distance from everyone. But she was watching everything: her eyes were brilliant and green, like two sticky boiled sweets.

It was as if Ada believed herself to be invisible, observing everyone.

In school, within those high walls, Ada kept her distance from Winnie, too. If they passed in the corridor or the schoolyard Ada would look at her friend blankly. At first Winnie had been offended by this. Oh, so I'm good enough for her when we're at home, when I can teach her her lessons and give up my time . . . But that wasn't it. Slowly, over years and years, Winnie came to realise that Ada wasn't being two-faced. Rather, in publicly pretending that they hardly knew one another, Ada was protecting her friend.

Ada was an outsider. Rough family, rough tongue. She would pass no exams, she'd curry no favour. She'd never get anywhere. The world had already given up on Ada Jones. She looked dirty and shabby; she smelled fusty and unwashed. Winnie knew that the girl did her best to keep herself clean and nice. She was fighting a losing battle, though. Living in that house, in that family. She brought her family's taint to school with her.

Winnie, on the other hand, was popular because she was average and normal as could be. She was the mumsy type. Neither beautiful, nor clever, she wasn't envied or despised by anyone. She wasn't stuck-up and she was respected because her mother was known by other people's mums as a decent woman. In fact, Winnie received commiserations now and then, for having to live next door to those dirty Jones people.

Sometimes it would infuriate Winnie that Ada kept her head down and mumbled when the teachers barked questions at her. How could she keep all her restless intelligence and energy squashed down all day long? Winnie knew that brilliant things were going on inside Ada's mind all the time: she was crackling and fizzing with ideas and stories and jokes. How come nobody could ever see that? Nobody seemed aware of the brilliance seeping out of her.

Ada managed to keep herself incognito. Winnie flinched and ducked whenever a teacher flung a wooden blackboard cleaner at Ada. Once it cracked off her collarbone, puffing up chalk dust. Winnie could see that it had really hurt her. The teacher had let his frustration push him too far. Ada bit her lip and refused to cry or complain. Steadfastly, Ada refused to give answers when the teachers asked even the most rudimentary questions. She refused to do homework. She refused to pass exams. And, eventually, because the other kids were so rowdy and demanding, and because there were so many of them, Ada slipped past the teachers' notice. She bided her time and left school, unqualified for everything, at the first possible opportunity.

'But why do you fail deliberately?' Winnie kept asking her, after school, over the years. 'You know more than any of them. You can write things down better than anyone.'

Ada tutted and rolled her eyes. Only once had she given Winnie an answer that rang true. 'They don't teach anything that's of any use to me,' she said. 'All their measurements and weights and chemistry and rats' guts. They turn everything into useless stuff you have to learn off by heart . . .'

On the very last day of school all of their year group had walked through the school gates with the slightly hunched, tense postures of prisoners of war being liberated from a camp: expecting a bullet between the shoulder blades at any moment. Thinking, surely, it can't be right? We can't be free to go . . .?

It was Ada who broke ranks first, of course. As she

reached the sand dunes she started to run. She clutched her battered leather satchel to her still-flat chest and she pelted into the bracing sea wind, kicking up plumes of stinging sand. She let out one huge roar, which startled everyone else.

Winnie laughed – at Ada, at everyone's faces – and she ran after her friend. She didn't care who saw they were friends. She had never cared about that. But now, maybe, with school over, Ada would no longer hold her at arm's length. Then, everyone else was too caught up in their own dramas of fleeing the schoolhouse for ever, to even notice that Winnie and Ada were running together, down to the beach, over the lumpen dunes. They were screaming together now, holding hands. Winnie's fingers were crushed in Ada's fierce grip, but she didn't care.

Winnie's satchel hadn't been fastened securely and she lost a few exercise books and pages of painstaking work. She even lost the sentimental sheet of autographs she had collected from teachers and staff of the school: all of these pages went careening away across the beach. Winnie didn't mind. She wasn't going back to school, either. She was no scholar, but she had the certificates that she needed. She had learned quite enough. Her mum had made it plain: it was about time that Winnie brought a bit of money home. She wasn't a child any more.

Finding a job would be easy. The Duchess was well known and respected in their part of town. She had contacts. Winnie would be a good worker, if she took after her mum. She was the dependable, homely type. Winnie wasn't flighty. She would never give anyone any trouble.

This was the next stage Winnie was looking forward to, that afternoon. She was imagining working in a shop on the high street. A job fixed up by an acquaintance of the Duchess's. Maybe in the big department store. Shoes, or corsets ... or the stationer's counter, perhaps. Creamy papers and the blue smell of ink.

Running along the seashore with Ada she could put that future out of her mind for a while, as they tore through the onrushing waves and swung their satchels round their heads.

She was plumper than Ada and out of breath sooner. She had to pause to heave in ragged breaths and hold her knees and, when she looked up again, Ada was still running. She was splashing through the foam and freezing salt water as it slid up the damp beach.

'Wait! Wait for me, Ada!' Winnie laughed, panting.

Ada didn't look back.

Limbs like pistons, she carried on running, just like Winnie knew she would.

Eleven

On the bus that Saturday morning, Simon was starting to wonder what Kelly had meant. What was this 'news' she reckoned she had for him? It was something to do with his gran, she'd said. Something they were going to do for her.

His gran certainly needed cheering up. She had hardly said a word this morning. Usually Winnie was a morning person: infuriatingly bright-eyed and bushy-tailed at breakfast time. Not today. She didn't even look that bothered about going to the Great Big Book Exchange. She had packed her shopping bag with last week's freight of novels, ready to give them back. Simon knew that she hadn't even finished them. Some of them she'd hardly looked at. All she'd read all week was Ada Jones.

His gran was getting depressed, he thought. She wasn't even enjoying her reading the same.

Outside, across the flat, muggy landscape, the weather was mirroring her gloom. The windows of the bus were running wet and the trees were getting battered leafless by the wind. It was foolhardy, going out to trot around the shops. Already Winnie's brolly had blown inside out, snapping several struts, as they'd walked to the bus stop. The whole day around them felt disastrous: like the worst, most ominous day to be out in.

But still Winnie and Simon were heading out for the Exchange. They hadn't even discussed the option of staying at home instead. Home, where it was cosy and dry and they could read their old books to their hearts' content.

Neither of them wanted to stay at home today.

They didn't want to be around Grandad.

Grandad had blown his top this morning. It had happened when he'd ambled over to put his breakfast plate and mug into the sudsy water of the sink. What he'd found there were all last night's supper dishes waiting for him. Around that stack there were floating islands of globby grey grease.

Ray had gone up in a blue light: lashing out furiously. His words hadn't even been coherent or clear enough for the others to make out what he was saying, but the sense of them was obvious. He was sick to his eye teeth of living in a filthy midden. Winnie – whose responsibility their home was – had let it go all to hell.

Winnie was sitting at the kitchen table with her mug of tea raised halfway to her mouth. She watched expressionless as Ray hopped and danced about like wicked Rumpelstiltskin. Her eyes hardened as she watched him screech and gesticulate. Perhaps she hoped he'd stamp a bit harder; stamp a hole in the ground and disappear for ever, just like Rumpelstiltskin had.

But Ray didn't disappear. Instead he hurried to the bookcase in the corner of the kitchen – one of many spill-over bookcases in the bungalow – and yanked out an armload of paperbacks. Before anyone could stop him, the old man whirled them around and dumped them unceremoniously into the sink of dishes and greasy cold water.

'There!' he cried. 'Filthy! Everything's filthy! How do you like it, eh? You dirty old woman! How do you like your dirty books now?'

Then he was picking up more books, plucking random volumes from the rickety shelves – cookery, science fiction, travel guides – and flinging them into the sink, so that grey slimy water sploshed everywhere and a rack of relatively clean dishes were dashed noisily to the lino.

Winnie and Simon took a few moments to react to this extraordinary display.

'What the devil . . .?' Winnie began, terrified. She got up and started to back away, staring at her books turning to mulch in the sink.

'Grandad . . .' Simon said warily, feeling useless. The damage was already done.

As always, quite abruptly, the wind went out of Grandad's sails. His mad, destructive fit passed by – quick as clouds across the moon on a stormy night. He stood stock-still with books still clutched to his chest, pages dropping out and drifting to the floor. He let the whole lot fall amongst the debris on the kitchen lino. 'Well,' he said, glaring at his wife and grandson. 'See? There's only so much I can take, you see. There's only so much mess and filth and chaos that I'll put up with.'

'Ray . . .'

He made a swift gesture with his hand, cutting Winnie off short. He didn't want to discuss anything with her.

'Ray,' she persisted.

'You're going to get rid of them,' he said darkly. 'You and the boy. You're going to get rid of your dirty old books. You hear me? I want them all out of my house.'

Now Winnie was coming out of her trance.

Since Ray's fit this morning she had been in a kind of stupor, perched meekly on the back seat of the bus beside

167

Simon. She hadn't wanted to discuss this morning's scene, or anything much at all. Simon didn't fancy talking about it either. He was starting to think that his gran might have been right. Grandad was losing his marbles. Who else would go into paroxysms over a few books piled up around the place?

He'll make you get rid of yours as well, Simon reminded himself. It's your grandad's house, after all. It's his name on the rent book. It's up to him who and what belongs there.

Once, when leaving his parents' home, Simon had thought himself content to get rid of his novels. To dump them, as just another redundant part of his lost, previous life.

Not now though. What Winnie had said to him back then was right. The novels he had read anchored him here, inside his life. They reminded him of who he was supposed to be. And of who he wanted to become.

He looked at Winnie as their bus finally made its way into Kelly's town. (It was funny, that was how he thought of the place now – like that was its name. Like Kelly was the most important thing there.) With a shock he realised that Winnie was close to tears.

'Don't mind me,' she said. 'I'm a silly old woman. Your

grandad's right. What's the point in getting upset over a bunch of old novels?'

The Book Exchange smelled wonderful and welcoming. They were used to its curious mixture of wood and old paper; the teasing aroma of strong coffee. Winnie and Simon hurried in out of the wet and gulped down this air as if it was medicine.

How many times had they visited here? Not many. Only a month or so ago they hadn't even known the place existed. Now it seemed as if every detail of these rooms was something Simon could see when he closed his eyes at night. He even imagined living in the flat above the Exchange, like the man with two plastic arms did. To Simon, that seemed like the best place in the world to live, with all these rooms beneath him. A labyrinth between himself and the world outdoors. Kelly guarding him, painting her fingernails black as she sat on her high stool. What did that make Kelly? he wondered. The Minotaur? He wasn't sure how she'd feel about that.

'Hiya,' she said, as he and his gran brought their books to the desk.

'Ah, my friends,' sighed Terrance, holding out both arms in greeting. 'Right on time, as usual. It's getting to be the highlight of my week, seeing you.'

Simon knew that by 'you' he meant Winnie. She moved towards him and it was clear, suddenly, that he was holding out both plastic arms for her to take hold of. Or maybe he was attempting to embrace her. It was hard to be sure. Winnie went up to him and, after a clumsy moment of hesitation, took hold of his fake hands and pressed his fingers, in greeting, as if he could really feel it. The Exchange owner flushed with gratification.

Simon and Kelly were watching with great interest.

Then, suddenly, Winnie burst into loud and messy tears. She startled even herself with the intensity of her sobbing. This made her even worse and soon she was wailing and her face went scarlet with frustration and fright.

Terrance darted an anguished look at his assistant. He tried to get Winnie to put her head on his shoulder, but she was taller than him, so it was awkward to manage. Then he tried to hug her, to pull her close and to pat and rub her back, but his fake hands weren't dextrous enough. He looked angry at his own uselessness and, all the while, Winnie continued to give vent to her sadness and her grief.

Simon had never seen anything like it. His gran never let go of her feelings. Not even at the funeral had she behaved like this. A dignified little sniffle. A stifled sob now and then. Sometimes a bit of a stomp about and a hissed, angry word.

But this display was melodrama; it was opera. It was unheard of in public.

After a while she subsided and Terrance lowered his useless, unfeeling arms. He turned away and hooked up his jacket from the back of his wooden chair and slipped it expertly on. 'I'm taking you out for a coffee,' he told Winnie, in a bright, extra-hearty fashion.

'What?' She pressed a wad of damp tissues to her eyes. Her face felt swollen and horrible.

'I'm going to treat you,' he said. 'We'll have cakes and buns and whatever else you want. It's about time you and I had a little sit-down together. Come on!' He was full of bravado. He wouldn't take no for an answer.

Winnie – Simon could tell – was flattered, embarrassed, horrified and pleased, all at the same time. 'I've made a show of myself in front of you . . .' she said.

'So?' Terrance smiled. 'Mop yourself up. It doesn't matter. Come along with me. Let's go and enjoy ourselves.' He proferred his arm again, so she could link with him.

Winnie threaded her arm through his very carefully, as if she was scared she might break him. Then they were heading for the main door, without a backward glance. Terrance called something back to Kelly about holding the fort, and Kelly replied helpfully, but Simon wasn't taking much of it in. He was still gobsmacked by his gran's upsetting collapse. He hadn't realised she was as close to the edge as that. And Terrance was waiting for her, at the moment she toppled over into despair. He had been so gallant.

'They are going to fall in love,' Kelly said, jolting Simon back to the present, timeless moment of the Exchange.

'What?'

'I knew it was going to happen,' she said.

Simon didn't say anything.

'I always know when stuff like that is going to happen,' she said, eyeing Simon.

Now they were alone together, for the first time since saying goodbye on the X50 Express. It felt weird to be alone with her in the Book Exchange. Weird but right. Like this place could be their own world. They could be self-sufficient here and never want for anything or anyone else. Simon allowed himself a few moments' fantasising in this vein. He wondered if all the books packed into these rooms could last him out the rest of his life. It wasn't a very practical fantasy, was it? he realised. Unless they could survive on coffee and custard creams they would be dead of starvation pretty soon. It was a stupid fantasy. Kelly was giving him a look like she knew what kind of stupid stuff was going through his mind.

'What's wrong with Winnie?' she asked. 'She must be really upset, if that's how she reacts to a bit of kindness.'

Simon knew she was right. It was Terrance holding out his arms like that. Attempting to reach for her with those plainly artificial hands. There was so much tenderness in that gesture. Somehow it had pitched Winnie over into that crying fit.

Quickly Simon explained about Grandad Ray that morning: the savagery of his behaviour; his destructiveness and threats; the way that kind of thing was becoming more frequent. The pall of anger and black depression that had started to hang over their bungalow just recently. As he said all of this, Simon realised that it was true. It *had* been pretty tense at home of late. They had all been living under a weird kind of pressure. Kelly was nodding sagely.

'Maybe it would be best if Winnie really did run off and leave him. It doesn't sound like they can go on much longer like they are.'

'But they've been together . . . for ever,' Simon said. 'They can't just split up now.'

'Why not?' Kelly smiled. 'Just because you can't imagine it? Because they're your gran and grandad and you can't picture them apart?'

'Of course not,' Simon snapped. What he didn't say,

though, was that he was starting to believe it was all his fault. His coming to live with them was what was causing all this tension. It was breaking them apart.

'Sometimes,' said Kelly, 'the worst thing you can imagine *has* to happen, in order for things to get better.'

Simon tutted. 'You sound like daytime TV.'

She swore at him. 'I think it's a good thing, if Winnie and Terrance fell in love. If she ran off with him. He wouldn't mind how many books she read. He'd make her happy. She'd be good for him. He's got no one now. No family left. She'd make all the difference.'

Simon was uncomfortable talking like this. Kelly was making Winnie sound like some kind of loose woman who went running off with the first bookshop owner she liked the look of. Was Winnie really that keen on escaping the life that she had? He wondered. She had spent all her time making her life into what it was. Would she willingly change all of it around?

Simon hated change. He knew that much about himself. Change was something that simply happened to you. You yourself didn't make change happen. Instead you were at its mercy. This past year had taught him that. Change could pick you up; it could pick up everyone and everything in your life and it could wantonly destroy and randomise every factor. It could dump your whole life down again, altered out of all recognition. Simon didn't want anything to change, ever again. Not without loads and loads of warning.

Suddenly he remembered what he had wanted to ask Kelly. 'What did you mean, when you phoned me? About doing something to cheer up my gran?' He was changing the subject, he knew. Kelly looked at him like he was being deliberately evasive. But now was the right time to cheer up Winnie. To do something that didn't involve her running off with a man with no arms.

'Oh,' said Kelly, opening a drawer in her desk and rooting around. 'I picked up a flyer in town. There's an event I think you'll want to go to. Quite soon. You'll want to take your gran.'

'An event?'

'A books event,' she said. 'What they're calling "a Literary Lunch"' . . . Ah. Got it.'

She passed him a slip of pink paper. On it there was a rather dark and smudgy reproduction of a photo of an elderly lady. She was scowling and, even though the photo was of terrible quality, there was a great intensity to her gaze. A certain twinkling wit shone through. What really attracted Simon's attention was the blocky print announcing a Literary Lunch at the King's Arms Hotel, and the identity of the

'Grand Guest of Honour – International Bestseller and Beloved Local Novelist – Ada Jones'.

It took a few moments to sink in. 'She's coming here,' he said. 'The King's Arms . . . that's here. That's in this town. Just off High Row.' He glanced at the date on the flyer. 'It's a week next Friday.' He looked up at Kelly, who was grinning.

'We have got to go, haven't we?' she said. 'We just have to spring it on your gran, don't we? It'll be amazing. She'll die of shock.'

Simon laughed. 'That's not exactly the desired effect.'

'You know what I mean. She'll be over the moon. She'll be so glad. Just imagine, Simon. Just picture it. After all these years. All this time. Reunited! Those two little girls, whose lives took them so far apart . . . in such different directions . . .'

Simon was thinking of the two little girls in that first Ada Jones novel, that he had been reading this past week. Despite the occasional mawkishness of the writing he had utterly succumbed to the tale of their growing up and growing apart. He had recognised his gran, too: even as a little girl, even in a novel. Ada had captured her. He shivered now, at the thought of being able to add another chapter, maybe, to that story. Imagine the two of them, he thought: Winnie and Ada coming face to face after all these years.

'The King's Arms is really smart,' Kelly said. 'It's a Christmas lunch they're doing. Come on, Simon. It'll be fab. Let's do it. They do all this gorgeous food and loads of wine and then Ada gets up and does a talk and afterwards we'll be able to go up to her and say: Look! Here's the little friend you knew when you were seven years old! Here's Winnie, who gave you your first notebook. She taught you to read and write, didn't she?' Kelly rolled her eyes and whistled through her teeth. 'I mean . . . Ada owes your gran everything, really.'

'Maybe Gran wouldn't want to go,' said Simon. 'Maybe she wouldn't want to embarrass Ada.'

'Are you kidding? Of course she'll want to. Let's do it, Simon. Let's buy the tickets.'

He flicked the pink flyer at her. 'Have you seen the cost? They're forty quid each. Just for lunch and the chance to gawp at some old wife.'

'It'll be all posh people going, that's why,' Kelly said. 'But we deserve to be there as much as they do, don't we? More than them, actually. Oh, come on, Simon. We could run down town right now and buy the tickets . . .'

'Hold on,' he said. 'Do you realise how much that is?'

'Well, there's me and you and your Gran . . . one hundred and twenty pounds.'

He pulled a face. Leaving aside the fact that he hadn't yet *offered* to buy a ticket for Kelly herself, it was still a lot of money to come out of his special account.

'Your insurance money,' Kelly urged him tactlessly. 'You told me you've got money in the bank. You can afford it.'

'It's not a huge amount,' he said.

'Enough for this?'

'Well, yes,' he said. 'But . . .' He looked down.

'What?'

'My grandad. He checks all my statements. He checks everything to do with that money. He didn't think I should have had access to it so soon. He thinks I'll waste it. I'm already waiting for him to go crackers over that fifty quid I blew the other day, when we bunked off school. That'll cause enough problems. I can't take out £120, just for lunch on another day when I should be at school.'

Kelly looked surprised. 'He checks your account?' she said. 'Wow. That's rough.'

'I suppose he doesn't trust me with it,' Simon said. 'He's the same with Gran. She has to give him receipts for everything.'

'Well,' said Kelly. 'We'll have to think of something else. Some way of getting the money out of your account without him knowing . . .'

She walked away from Simon, playing with her hair thoughtfully. Simon watched her go, sucking in a lungful of patchouli-scented air as she passed. The sharpness of the air stung his sore lip. He sighed. He wasn't even sure this literary lunch event was a good idea at all. It was the kind of thing he could very well imagine ending up in disaster. Kelly was taking it as read, though, that he was in agreement with her: that they would be willing to move heaven and earth in order to bring Winnie back into Ada's glamorous orbit.

'Where are you going?' Simon suddenly asked Kelly, realising that she'd wandered off into the next book-lined room. He went after her.

'Come and see,' she said, laughing. She was leading him into the labyrinth. Ariadne – that's who she was.

'Where?' he asked, and then realised.

'Behind the beaded curtain,' she said. Then there came a percussive clatter and tinkle of coloured beads. 'This is our chance, while the others are away,' she said. 'Why don't you come into the room that you didn't even know existed . . .?'

Twelve

Simon was starting to feel peculiar. The air here seemed heavier, thicker with dust. It was darker, too. Just two amber bulbs sent out a very murky light into the cupboard-like space of the secret room. Kelly stood wordlessly beside him, watching him absorb the details of the place.

The walls were decorated with old magazines preserved in plastic bags. The women on the covers were familiar to him. They had the same jaunty, ooh-la-la expressions; the same dayglo tans and the same ruffly bikinis. These were the same compliant faces that had stared out of his grandad's collection of mags.

What was it about these men and their secrets? These hidden stashes, treasures in the attic, these unnoticed rooms. It was as if this clandestine stuff was a part of growing up and becoming a man. Simon was starting to wonder: would becoming a man mean he would have to be the same as that?

Would he have to learn to keep secrets of his own? To be shifty like that?

Just being in this stale-smelling room, Simon felt like he was examining Terrance's private belongings, rather than just another part of his shop.

He stared at the pert and nubile models. These dolly birds from the past. He looked up at this array of bums and breasts with polite interest and he could hear Kelly smirk at him. He was looking at these women like he would at the bouncing cherubs of the Sistine Chapel. But that's how he felt. Pretty much unmoved by the whole thing.

'How am I supposed to feel?' he asked, and realised that he was speaking aloud. 'Sexy?'

'I think these pictures are quite sexy,' said Kelly, flipping through the racks of magazines. 'I can see what some of these old men like about them.' She shrugged. 'I'll tell you what makes me feel weird, though. And that's how old these pictures are. These young women could now very well be wrinkly, saggy old women. They could be the age of your gran . . .'

'Stop it,' Simon laughed, but feeling at the same time, vaguely offended on his gran's behalf.

'What if she was in here somewhere?' Kelly went on. 'What if she had an earlier career as a glamour model, eh?'

'That's the kind of thing that would happen in a novel,'

said Simon. 'We'd look at one of these mags, and there she'd be . . .'

'In an Ada Jones novel,' said Kelly. 'That's what would happen. Some sensational secret from the past, breaking out into the present.'

'You're right,' he said. 'But that's not what happens in real life, is it? Not our lives, anyway.' Simon glanced around again. 'Can we go back to the shop, now? I'm feeling a bit oppressed by all this heaving female flesh everywhere.'

'Some men would relish that.'

'I feel like I'm running out of oxygen.'

She snorted. He looked round at her and, in the smoky orange lighting, her make-up looked more bizarre than ever. Not unattractive, but sort of hellish and extreme. Her eyes were almost completely black. Her jagged fringe cast long, spiky shadows down her weirdly pale skin. The hollow of her throat looked very soft and white.

'Do you want to kiss me again?' she said. 'You messed it up when you tried last time.'

'When *I* tried?' he burst out. 'You were the one lunging at me!'

'That's not how I remember it.'

He was stung by the injustice of this. 'That's not true. That's not what happened.'

Exchange

'No?'

'No! I would never have—'

'Oh, great,' she said. 'Cheers. You'd never have tried to kiss me. How come? Am I that revolting?'

'No!' He was flustered. 'I just mean I wouldn't have jumped on you, on the bus, like that.'

She shrugged. 'Oh well. Your loss. It was a lousy kiss anyway.'

He nodded. He felt a rush of sadness. Suddenly there was even less space between them in this murky room. He grew anxious and conscious of all the nipples and buttocks and pouting lips.

In here he felt illicit. He felt like they were somewhere they shouldn't be. It added an extra spice to the melange of scents and sensations in the Book Exchange.

Kelly had brought him here for a reason. All of a sudden Simon felt like he was undergoing a kind of test. It made him feel confused. He glanced up at a calendar of nudists from 1958. Pale pink women were springing about, energetically playing volleyball; their hair frosted with lacquer and their private parts airbrushed out of sight. None of it made him feel sexy. Was it supposed to? Was that what Kelly had been intending?

Swiftly he turned and lowered his head to kiss her. He

took her by surprise so that she cried out and he ended up with a mouthful of sticky hair. 'Oww! Simon . . .!' She pushed him away. 'What are you—?'

'I was having another go!' he protested, rubbing his tongue on his shirtsleeve. 'Your hair gel tastes foul.'

'That was rubbish,' she said. 'You call that kissing? That's twice now, you've got it all wrong. You'll end up banging our heads together and knocking us senseless. You've got no sense of timing. You're completely out of synch with me. What is it, have you never kissed anyone before?'

He was colouring up. He looked down at his trainers. 'Um,' he said. 'Well, no.'

'You've never had a girlfriend? Never practised on anyone? Round the bike sheds at school?'

He shook his head. Kelly bit her lip, looking ashamed at the way she had bawled him out. She shouldn't have criticised his technique. He didn't *have* a technique! It had taken him all his courage to push himself forward, pucker up his lips and go in to plant one on Kelly's black-painted mouth. He groaned with shame.

'Simon,' she said, as he turned to duck back through the glass-beaded curtain. 'Come back.'

'No, thanks,' he said. She had humiliated him in front of

those nude, volleyball-playing lovelies. He could almost imagine them, giggling behind his back.

Kelly caught up with him in the main room of the Exchange.

'You left everything unattended,' he said. 'Anyone could have come in and looted the place.'

She shrugged. 'Hardly anyone ever comes in. It's like hardly anyone knows we're here.'

'My gran will be back soon,' he said, though he had no idea whether that was true or not. He couldn't look Kelly in the eye. 'I'm going to choose some books,' he said.

'Simon, look. I'm sorry,' she said. 'I'm sure you're a great kisser, when you get the hang of it. Because you're sensitive and lovely and you've got those soft, full lips . . .'

'Shut up,' he said, squirming.

'I'd love you to kiss me properly,' she said. 'But the time's just not been right. We haven't got it right yet. Maybe we will. Maybe we won't. But I'm sorry I yelled. You just gave me a surprise back there. Eating my hair.'

He pulled a face.

'Oh, come on,' she said. 'Lighten up! Look – it was my fault. I'm jumpy. I'm twitchy. I'm nervous as well.'

'What of?' he said.

'I don't know. But . . . I like you, Simon.'

He nodded. 'Me too. I mean, you. I like you.'

'Good,' she said.

'Can we shut up about it for now?' he asked, wincing.

She nodded. 'You go and find some books. But first, let me tell you about my idea.'

He frowned. 'What kind of idea is it?'

'About getting money. For our tickets. For the Ada Jones Literary Lunch.'

'Oh, that again . . .' he said. 'Maybe we shouldn't bother.'

'We have to,' said Kelly. 'And from what I hear, Ada won't be around for ever. She's been very ill. Her publishers are saying this is the last big publicity tour she'll ever do. If we ever want to see her and if your gran wants to see her again, then we have to do this, Simon. A slap-up lunch a week on Friday! We just have to!'

He was starting to picture it. It would be Christmas, suddenly. He put the three of them into lavish surroundings. Wonderful food and tinkling, soft music. And a reunion in the offing.

Something his mum had once said was coming back to him. 'Even if you have nothing left to show for it afterwards, you should never regret spending money on having a wonderful time. Even if all you'll have are your memories of that day. At least it's a day you will always remember. And just think how many other days simply sink into oblivion! Just how many days are completely forgettable . . .'

Of course – his mum's advice now would be that they would have to go. She'd be standing there, agreeing with Kelly. The two of them would be nodding solemnly. They'd be bonded together in agreement. So maybe the two of them would have got on, after all.

'I've an idea how we can get the money, too,' Kelly said, her eyes glinting.

'I've already told you,' he protested. 'My grandad goes through all my bank statements and my receipts. He'd hit the roof, soon as he saw I'd spent £120 like that. It's bad enough spending money on books. He resents even that. But this . . .!'

Kelly smiled. 'I've thought of something else. I've thought of a way we can raise the cash. Actually, I'm surprised you haven't thought of it yourself.'

'What? How?'

Kelly walked back to her stool by the cash desk. 'Your grandad's glamour mags. You should smuggle them out of his den. They'll be worth a fair bit, from what you've said. Terrance would give you a good price for them. He's very fair.'

Simon stared at her. His mouth fell open. 'Steal them? Steal them from my own grandad?'

'Why not?'

'I thought you liked him! You thought he was a nice old bloke. Why would you want to steal from him?'

'He's a bully,' Kelly said. 'He's bullied your gran for years. He's stood in the way of her happiness – that's how I see it. He deserves to be taught a lesson. He needs to take part in the Exchange . . .'

Simon was reeling. This was proper theft Kelly was suggesting. But, even as his mind went spinning, Simon was going over all the possibilities and ramifications. Could they really do it? And maybe they could even make it look like a burglary . . . He shook his head. What was he thinking of? Thieving off his own grandad! Who had taken him in and given him a home . . .

Kelly continued. 'Just think what it would mean to Winnie. Seeing Ada Jones again. Just before old Ada dies.' Kelly fixed Simon with a hard stare. 'You should do everything you can to make it happen. Look. I'll help you. I'll do everything I can to help you.'

He wasn't sure. It seemed like a really bad idea.

As the days went past, it seemed like an even worse idea.

He tried to forget it. He tried to ignore Kelly's messages. He deleted the texts from her: the ones that flashed up green on his mobile, urging him to action. Telling him that they were running out of time. If they were going to do it, then they had to get on with it. They had to raise the money. They had to buy their tickets. This was the Ada Jones farewell tour. The places at the lunch would be selling out rapidly.

He imagined Christmas place settings, with candles flickering and sprigs of mistletoe and holly.

He didn't reply to her. He couldn't do it. Steal from his grandad? It was a nasty idea. A cruel and selfish one. Simon watched his gran and grandad going about their everyday routines and he realised that they were living in their own separate bubbles. They might look as if they occupied the same bungalow and came to sit at the same table to eat Winnie's plain, homely food, but actually they were operating in two distinct dimensions. They had come unstuck and, these days, they each hardly seemed to notice the other's mood.

Which, Simon reflected, was probably just as well. Grandad was more erratic and sulky than ever. He was out every evening down the Legion, too. As if he had decided he could no longer bear being in the living room with Simon and Winnie. He came home after closing each night. Simon grew used to hearing the latch of the garden gate clashing and his gran jerking upright in her chair, determined to carry on reading as Ray swayed back into the room.

Winnie's mood was peculiar that week. Her depression had seemingly lifted. A little, anyway.

'We had the most wonderful, exotic coffee,' she said. 'With chocolate in it and all this whipped cream on top. And cakes like you've never seen, Simon. It was like being in Vienna or somewhere. These great big things all heaped up and slathered in icing sugar and even more cream. And Terrance just said, "Eat up, Winnie! I hope you don't go counting the calories like all those other foolish women."' Winnie blinked and grinned, coming out of her reverie. 'He said I was perfect, Simon. He said I was the perfect example of a woman in my prime.'

Simon thought that was maybe pushing it a bit. But there could be no doubt about the fact that Terrance had been determined to flatter and impress Winnie. He was wooing her, Simon thought. He was wooing her with gateaux and frothy mochas and the tender ministrations of his plastic hands . . .

'What else?' he asked his gran, as they ate supper together. His grandad wasn't there to eat with them. This was the first time that he had missed a meal, staying in the pub. At first his plate steamed, untouched, at the head of the kitchen table. Winnie jumped up to put it in the oven, and then she described her cafe jaunt with Terrance in a hushed tone and even greater detail.

'I don't know what else to say,' she said, looking bewildered. 'We talked. We talked about all kinds of things. It was nice. To have someone else to talk to.' She caught his eye and reached out to pat his hand. 'Oh, I know I talk to you, lovely. But you know what I mean. Someone of my own ancient years. And he talked to me like a real person. He wanted to know all about me. Well, imagine! I didn't know where to start. I told him, there's nothing to tell. I've never really done anything. The most exciting thing I ever get up to is reading all these novels and finding out what exciting things all the other people get up to. . . And he laughed at that, Simon. Not nastily. Not in a belittling way. Do you know what he said?'

'What?'

'He said that he's the same. He's lived all his life in books. He says that most of the people he knows don't really exist at all. And they're more vital, more alive than the real people he sees. He says he only loves those people who aren't meant to be real . . .'

'It all sounds a bit weird to me,' said Simon. He realised that he was sounding more cynical than he wanted to.

'He sort of put me in a trance,' said Winnie. 'Next thing

I knew, I was asking a really personal question. I said, did he
think it was easier to love people in books, than in real life?
He looked at me and he's got these marvellous eyes.
Haunting. Almost yellow where they should be white. The
irises are nearly orange, like a tiger. Those eyes of his blazed
at me. And he said that characters in novels never leave you,
and they never die. You've got them for ever. They can't
come to any real harm. Even if they die, at the end of their
story, you can always turn back to the start and there they are
again. Large as life, and talking and breathing once more.'
Winnie stopped toying with her mostly untouched dinner
and put her knife and fork down neatly, at the half-past six
position on her plate. 'I said that it wasn't the same. I didn't
think it sounded healthy. I told him that even I – with all the
reading that I get caught up in – well, even I know that it
isn't really real. The people in the books aren't more real
than the people in my life, and my family around me.'

'What did he say?'

A shadow seemed to pass across Winnie's face. 'He just
said, "What about Ada Jones?"'

'What did he mean by that?'

'I'd told him I'd started reading her books in order, properly. To reacquaint myself with the Ada I used to know. And
he just said, "Well? Isn't she real to you from your reading?

Isn't the Ada from the books more real now than your memories?"'

'Wow,' said Simon. 'That's heavy.'

'I thought about it, and it was true! I thought about moments from the past, like when I first met Ada and when she came round our house to write, and I realised that what I was remembering came from her novel, and not from my head at all. The books were realer than real life.'

As Simon absorbed this, and started to turn the thought over, they both heard the garden gate rattle and then crash open. Winnie shot Simon a look. He knew it meant: let's drop this subject now. Don't talk about any of this in front of your grandad.

When Grandad Ray appeared in the kitchen, looking mithered and wobbly on his feet, Simon thought: my gran is behaving like a woman embarking on an affair. Already she sounds like she is falling furtively in love. All they have done is eat some cake and talk about weird stuff. Weird stuff that made Simon slightly dizzy.

He watched his gran get up and bustle and cluck around Grandad. ('Leave off, woman! I'm not hungry now!' 'You've got to eat! All that drink on an empty stomach! Look, I've done fish fingers and crinkle-cut chips! They're not too dried up in the oven . . . Sit yourself down, Ray!')

Simon watched them, feeling very removed from the scene. He thought: if I was to write down everything I knew about my mum and dad, now, while it's still all there in my memory . . . if I was to write it all down, in the kind of detail like you get in a novel – would that make *them* real again? Realer than they are now in the real world? Well, they're nothing here now, are they? They don't exist any more. They've gone. And if I were to write about them and do everything I could to conjure them up . . . Would that bring them back? Just a little bit? Even if it's just in a small way, a fake way . . . Would that count?

He didn't know. He really didn't know.

He watched his surly grandad, chomping on dried-up fish fingers. His grandad glared past him.

What's the point of reading, if I can't write back?

What's the point of knowing unreal people, if they aren't the ones I want to know?

Who do I want to know? he thought. Who do I want to be with?

He imagined sitting with loads of blank paper, his pen twitching, eager, but unable to start. Unable to think up a perfect first sentence. He imagined trying to bring them – to bring anyone – to life.

Thirteen

Kelly was talking like what they were planning was a bank heist. Her texts and her messages had become very terse and serious. It was ridiculous, in a way – all this fuss over a box of old magazines – but it all made Simon feel quite nervous. Kelly was plotting and planning and he was being swept along in it all. He wasn't brave enough to stop her and to make her call it off.

He lay in his narrow bed at night and imagined that box of saucy mags, snug in their hidey-hole, up in the rafters. They exerted a strange pressure on him. If he was to go along with Kelly's plan, would they get away with it? What if they were caught? When would Grandad realise that his boxful of sunbathing beauties had absconded?

He was Bluebeard, of course, with his garage of wives from bygone years.

Simon was nervous because he knew, really, that they had

to do this. He had to get his gran to this literary lunch. Something had clinched it for him. Their conversation, perhaps, about how the books were now more real than Winnie's memory. Simon wanted Winnie to meet Ada again and see that that was wrong. The real person was still there. The memories were still strong.

It was as if, in this way, Simon would be proving something to himself. Something about his own memories of his mum and dad. He wanted to know that he could keep them both alive inside his own mind.

Novels are just a shadow world, he told himself. They're not as real as anything that happens here. Even if someone is dead, they are still more real than a character in a book.

He lay in his dim, chilly room, thinking this and trying to convince himself. The stacks of books around him looked like towers and skyscrapers looming over him.

He woke in the same position, with the sun gleaming weakly through the narrow, net-curtained window. It was December now and, even without checking, he knew that it had turned frosty overnight.

His gran was whipping up scrambled eggs in a hot skillet, tapping her moccasins to something on Radio 2. 'You've got a parcel, look,' she said.

It was by his breakfast plate. Obviously book-shaped.

Brown paper and string, which seemed affected and old-fashioned. It was addressed in scrawled Gothic lettering that he just knew was Kelly's. He recognised her elaborate script from his Exchange membership card.

'How nice,' Winnie grinned, bringing toasted muffins and eggs and peering over his shoulder at the vintage thriller Kelly had posted him. The cover was lurid with moonlight, bats and scratchy branches. 'I wish somebody would send *me* parcels like that.' She patted his shoulder. 'It must be something she wants you to read urgently, if it can't wait till Saturday. . .'

Simon waited till his gran beetled off to sort out her own breakfast, before he opened the note Kelly had poked inside the collection of mystery and adventure stories. The note was written in silver on purple sugar paper:

Sunshine –
Face it. You need my help to do this. Your nerve will
fail. You'll get a fit of conscience. So you need me –
heartless me – to help make it look like thieves have
been in and nicked your grandad's precious hoard.
(Or is that horde? Dunno.) Anyway, I'm not giving
you any chance to wimp out of this, kiddo. I'm
coming round your way tonight (Wednesday! You

should have this parcel with you on Weds morning. Yes?) and I'll help you smuggle out the booty while your grandad's down the pub. OK? You know it's the right thing. Your gran's need is greater than his, I reckon. OK? OK. See you tonight. I'll get there just after six.

XXXX K

Kisses, he thought. He was surprised she had put kisses at the end. He wondered if they were the failed and useless kind, when you ended up clashing teeth. Or were they the kind that made you horribly self-conscious? Or the ones where you ended up with a mouthful of hair? Also, kisses done like XXXX seemed a bit ordinary for her. He'd have expected something a bit more Gothic and unique from her. Grinning skulls and crossbones, maybe.

'Ahh,' said his gran, sitting down opposite. 'That Kelly's good to you, isn't she? She must think a lot of you, popping little presents in the post.'

'Hm,' said Simon, quickly folding the note back into the book. 'Look, I'd better get ready for school. I'm late already.'

'Eat your eggs first,' she warned.

He nodded. 'Kelly might come round tonight.'

'Oh! I've got nothing in . . .'

'It's not a special occasion,' he said, sounding terser than he meant to. 'She's just coming round to . . . hang out.'

'Hang out, eh?' Winnie laughed. 'Is that what the kids are doing nowadays? Well – so long as it's not hanging round the phone box, like that other rough lot. Though I know you and Kelly aren't like that. You two are so sensible and grown up. I can't believe how well behaved and considerate you both are . . .'

Yeah, right, thought Simon unhappily, gobbling up his breakfast as quickly as he could. And here we are, preparing to rob my grandad blind.

That day he felt like a stranger inside his own body. He was an alien in possession of this feeble human form and he was peering out of its eyes, mostly uninterested in the doings of these immature Homo sapiens.

He sat as near to the back as he could in all his classes, forever hoping to escape notice. He breathed in that terrible school-smelling fug of bleached lino, sweat and unwashed hair, chewing gum, and fags and farts. The lessons passed in a blur – his pen stirring at the page in a pretence of making salient notes. It was like writing in mollasses. In his History class he read Ada Jones under his desk. He was careless enough to be caught and his teacher – a wiry young man with a whiney, nasal voice and sweat patches in his grey shirt – snatched the book off him and held it up, sneeringly, in front of the class.

'What's this? You'd rather read old ladies' romantic books than listen to me, Jeffrey?' (This particular teacher never got anybody's name right.) 'What kind of thing is this for a young man of sixteen to be reading?'

Simon stared down at his desk, at all the graffiti scored deeply, angrily, into the varnished wood. He could feel the eyes of his classmates on him. They were starting to laugh – incredulous, disgusted, that a lad like him could be reading some old lady's book. A book about love.

'I don't know, Jeffrey,' the History teacher persisted. 'You don't really fit in here, do you?'

Later that afternoon he was humiliated in front of his classmates all over again in his English lesson, as it became clear that the teachers must have been discussing his curious case in the staffroom at lunchtime.

'Ada Jones, Simon?' laughed his English teacher, a plump, ironic woman he usually found quite encouraging. 'I wasn't aware that the exam board had put her on our syllabus . . .?'

'I was reading it for myself,' he said quickly. He couldn't

look at the teacher. He looked out at the playing fields and the woods beyond, through the wall of plate glass. A mist was coming down, rolling over the frozen grass, bringing more frost. It was a deathly landscape. A haunted scene.

'I'm all in favour of your reading novels for pleasure,' smiled the teacher. She smiled at all of them, taking them all in with a lighthouse-like beam. 'But really, I think you should all stick to literature. Don't read trash. It's a waste of your time. There's nothing to be learned from that stuff. Stick to the classics, to the quality stuff. And if you need to know which is which, ask me. I'll tell you. That's what I'm here for.' She gave one more grin, to close the subject.

Simon continued to gaze out of the window, as the details of the view smudged and faded under the pressure of the mist.

'Now,' said the teacher. 'If you fetch out your course handbooks and turn to the short extract on page twelve . . .'

Today he was dragging his feet going home. Usually he would hurry. Usually he would get across that field, and down the cinder path, and up the hill past the row of shops to his grandparents' street as soon as he could. He'd be deleting each chunk of his latest day at school as fully as he could: clicking and dragging each wearisome, torturous hour, and dumping them in the waste bin. Tonight he wasn't as keen on getting home.

Kelly was coming round and he wasn't looking forward to it. She was going to arrive and they were going to do something decisive and – he thought – wrong. He felt he couldn't back out of it now. He dawdled. He let all of the other kids brush past him, ignoring him. He stepped in every frozen puddle, just to hear the satisfying crack of ice. He counted the Christmas trees that had started to appear in neighbours' windows. They looked innocently gaudy.

But at last he was home again.

'Your friend's coming round again, isn't she?' Winnie smiled. 'Well, listen. Your grandad's going out, as usual, down the Legion. Don't tell him, but why don't I let the two of you "hang out" in your room, eh? Have a little privacy. Your grandad wouldn't like it, but I think you can be trusted.' She looked embarrassed. 'All right, Simon?'

He wished Kelly would whisper more quietly.

She was standing on the arm of Grandad's chair, with her head poking up into the rafters of the garage. She was telling him a tale, hissing it through her teeth, all indignant, as he weighed down the armchair so it couldn't tip. He was hoping that they wouldn't be heard. He was sure he would start sneezing or coughing, in all the dust that Kelly was dislodging.

'So there they were, soon as I got off the bus,' she was telling him, wrestling with the corner of the box. 'I'd forgotten all about them, of course. But they hadn't forgotten about me. Specially the one I smacked in the face last time. Anyway, straight away, they start yelling at me, just like they yell at you. Well, no offence, Simon, but if you get shouted at in the street and do nothing about it, everyone's gonna think you're soft . . .' She grunted loudly as she heaved at the box (how come she was taking so long?) and Simon winced. 'So I went over to them and their precious phone box and I asked them if they had a problem. They were really mouthy again, calling me a witch and everything and slagging you off, calling you a puff and all that, except that their leader didn't say much. He was a bit more . . . circumspect.' She let out a cry of triumph as the box came free of the rafters and she swayed backwards and almost fell. Simon grabbed one of her legs. 'It's OK,' she laughed. 'Anyway, they wouldn't stop shouting, so I punched him again.' She dropped the heavy box into Simon's waiting arms. He staggered a bit and the dust stung his eyes.

'You what? You punched him again?'

'Exactly the same as before.' Kelly dusted her hands.

'These people never listen, you see, Simon. And they never learn.'

'So you've just got to keep punching them in the face?'

Kelly nodded. 'It always works. For some silly, sexist reason, they don't expect it from a girl. So, down he went, all his brainless mates clustered round him, and off I skipped, merrily on my way, and here I am. *Voilà*!'

Simon opened the box to check it was the right one. All the while he was thinking: she's marvellous. And: I wish I was more like her. Now, this was a novel thought. He'd have to go over it, later. No time now.

'We have to get this lot out of here.'

'There must be about fifty mags in that box. Terrance will definitely give us enough cash . . .'

Simon grimaced, hating to be reminded of what they were doing. 'Come on,' he said. 'Let's get on with it.'

'That's some collection your grandad's got,' said Kelly. 'He must have had them for years.'

'Don't rub it in,' Simon snapped.

'Don't get me wrong,' said Kelly. 'I think he should get rid of them. For his own sake, as well as Winnie's. It's the ethos of the Great Big Book Exchange, isn't it? Don't hang on to stuff. Return it to the Exchange. Let other people share . . .'

'Hmm,' murmured Simon. He knew they were bending those benign rules somewhat.

Suddenly they both froze. At precisely the same moment, just as they were both crouching and holding the heavy box between them, they heard the noise. They stared at each other.

They had heard the sound of the garden gate clattering open. They heard the crash and tinkle of the milk bottles and one of them getting haphazardly smashed as Grandad came home, the worse for wear.

'It's not closing time,' Simon hissed. 'He's early.' He found he couldn't move. He was weighted down to the cement floor, as if by the box of glamour mags and Kelly's frantic stare.

'Will he come straight in here?' she asked.

'He might do. If he doesn't want to talk to Gran . . .'

Kelly cursed.

They heard the kitchen door slam; the metallic rattling of the venetian blinds. They heard the falsely jolly warbling of Winnie, greeting her husband. She's giving us time, Simon thought, amazed. Good old Gran! She thinks she's buying us time and giving us fair warning that Grandad's home early. Just because she thinks we're in my room, kissing or something. Gran doesn't know we're in here . . . stealing stuff.

'Quick,' said Simon. 'My room. Now! She's holding him off!'

Grandad's voice, coarsened and thickened with drink, seemed to reverberate through the plasterboard walls of the bungalow. He was drunkenly arguing the toss with Winnie. This was becoming a nightly occurrence. Simon didn't have time to listen and figure out what they were quarrelling over. He and Kelly were shuffling sideways to the interior door and lugging their stolen goods with them.

'He's coming . . .' Kelly gasped, as they hauled the box into Simon's room. They shut the garage door, heaved the box out of the way, and Simon flung his candlewick bedspread and his and Kelly's coats messily on top for camouflage.

'He has to come through my room to get to his garage,' said Simon. 'He never uses the front door.'

'I know,' said Kelly. 'I figured that out.'

From deeper in the bungalow they could hear doors clashing and Grandad yelling something incoherent at Winnie as he stomped away from her. He was heading in their direction, no doubt about it. They had only a matter of seconds.

'Get down on the bed,' Kelly commanded Simon.

'What?' He couldn't believe it. This was the absolute worst thing she could suggest. Before he could kick up a fuss, though, she had pounced on him and pinned him to his own mattress. He lay crumpled up in the sheets and half smothered by his pillows and Kelly was somehow, suddenly, sitting astride him and then her mouth was clamped down on his.

She was kissing him. Swiftly, expertly, and this time it worked. The surprise of it worked: leaving him helpless and open to this; to her tongue thrust incredibly, probingly, into his mouth. Oh, he thought, what if I bit it off out of shock?

Then his bedroom door flew open.

'What's this?' cried his grandad and Kelly withdrew her tongue before Simon's fears came true. She looked up at Grandad Ray and Simon craned his neck to watch upside down, sheepishly, as his grandad surveyed the chaos of the ransacked room.

He caught me on my bed with a girl, Simon groaned. Now I'll really pay for this.

'Whoops,' said Kelly mildly.

Simon's grandad's voice in reply was surprisingly measured and quiet. 'You might very well say "whoops", young lady. What's the meaning of all this?'

Kelly was up on her feet now, smoothing down her complicated layers of black clothing. She was putting on an extremely good act of looking penitent, Simon thought, as he sat up on the bed.

'Sorry, Grandad,' Simon stammered. 'It will never happen again.'

'I'm afraid we . . . got carried away, Mr Thompson,' said Kelly boldly.

Grandad Ray's eyes widened slightly. Simon couldn't be sure, but he thought maybe a smile was twitching at the corner of the old man's mouth. 'Carried away, eh?' he said, and glared at them both severely. 'You both know I won't have this kind of carry-on under my roof. Your gran trusted you, Simon, to behave properly. She tells me you gave her your word.'

Simon hung his head. He was aware of Kelly smirking at him. He was being treated like a child. But he was also aware of something gloating and pleased-sounding in his grandad's tone, even as he was berating him. Of course. That was it. Through all of this, even though he felt he had to behave crossly, Grandad Ray was actually delighted. He had caught Simon snogging a girl in his room. There was nothing wrong with Ray's grandson! Nothing at all! And, secretly, Grandad Ray was cock-a-hoop. This was cause for celebration! It was a rite of passage! Simon couldn't bring himself to look at either Kelly or Ray. He felt he'd turn purple with either embarrassment or confusion.

'Now, this isn't the kind of behaviour that Simon's gran

or I appreciate,' Ray told Kelly sternly. 'I hope you will both be more responsible in future. I suggest you catch your next bus home, Kelly. I think you've seen quite enough of Simon as it is, for this evening.'

She smiled sweetly at Simon's grandad. 'Yes, Mr Thompson.'

The old man even chuckled at her – her demure cheekiness – and he nodded and went back to the kitchen to tell Winnie what he had discovered.

Simon groaned. 'Look what you've done!' He sighed heavily. It was odd. He could still taste her kiss. Peppermints and patchouli oil.

Kelly picked up her coat. 'Oh, never mind. This will improve your reputation no end.'

'Reputation! They'll think I'm some kind of . . . sex beast.'

'Ha!' Kelly yanked the bedspread off the box of magazines. 'Some chance.' Then she hefted up the box. 'Aren't you going to help me onto the bus with these?'

'You'll never get them out of the house,' he said. 'You'll never get past the two of them.'

Kelly thought quickly. 'Give me that big bag,' she said, pointing at the bag where Simon kept the grungiest and nastiest of his dirty linen. Oh. Now she was going to see all of that as well. This was just about the most nerve-wracking and humiliating evening of his life.

Like a Gothic Santa Claus carrying her sack the colour of blackest night, Kelly left their bungalow waving a friendly goodnight. Poor Grandad Ray didn't have a clue she was taking a good number of his favourite, vintage magazines with her. She couldn't carry them all. Simon would have to return some to the garage. They would just have to hope this sackful would raise enough cash for their tickets. And they would have to hope that the bag wouldn't rip and disgorge its shocking contents.

Simon, still blushing from Kelly's emptying out the bag and seeing his pants and socks and T-shirts, had their cover story ready for when they carried the bag through the kitchen. There, Winnie was serving hot black coffee to sober Grandad up. He was still chuckling and there was a relaxed truce between the oldies. Both were enjoying the tale of Grandad walking in on Simon and Kelly as they kissed. There was a sense of relief to their pleasure – he's growing up properly. He isn't damaged or traumatised. Nothing has gone wrong with the boy.

'What's all this?' Grandad Ray asked, nodding at the black bag they were carrying between them.

'It's . . . books,' Simon huffed and puffed, opening the back door. 'Kelly's offered to take away a whole load of paperbacks I don't really want any more. I'm clearing some space, and getting rid of books I don't need, Grandad. Like you said we should.'

'What?' cried Winnie, whirling round with the coffee pot. 'But you must have dozens of them in that great big bag!'

Simon shrugged. 'Kelly has to catch her bus now . . .'

'Bye, Mr and Mrs T,' Kelly said, shuffling along.

'Let me have a look first,' Winnie said. 'Before you take them all to the Exchange. Let me check there's nothing I'd like to keep . . .' She'd put down the pot and was hurrying over.

'Leave them be, Winnie,' snapped Grandad Ray. 'The boy obviously knows his own mind. And he's made it up, to do what his Grandad Ray has told him. He's doing the right thing. He's getting rid of some of that old rubbish.'

As Grandad's words sank in, Simon and Kelly exchanged a glance. Ray was more correct than he knew. Meanwhile Winnie was standing there helpless, in the middle of the kitchen, wringing a tea towel in frustration.

'I'd better catch my bus,' Kelly said, and they went out.

On their way to the bus stop the two of them didn't get any hassle at all from the kids at the phone box. The leader had gone home early and the gang's remnants were muted and looked away from Kelly and Simon as the two of them went by, hauling their contraband to the bus stop.

When the bus came Simon helped lug the bag aboard.

'That looks like you've got a dead body in there,' said the driver cheerfully. 'I shall have to charge you double.'

Kelly scowled at him and flashed her student bus pass. 'Look, Simon, I'll text you before Saturday,' she said. 'I'll let you know how much I get for this lot.'

'Kidnappers!' laughed the bus driver. 'That's what you two are. What's in the bag?'

Kelly shrugged. 'Just some old rubbish. OK. See you soon, sunshine.'

She went to sit down and Simon stepped back onto the pavement, and it was only when the bus was gone that he realised that they hadn't kissed goodbye. He was surprised to find that he wished they had.

Fourteen

He had to wait a couple of days until Kelly texted him. Simon was on tenterhooks thinking: how did we imagine we'd get away with it? Grandad is bound to go looking up in the rafters for his magazines. We didn't even bother making it look like a burglary. We dropped that complicated part of the plan. So now, when he discovers their loss, he's bound to realise it's me who's been in and taken his private things.

What would he say?

Yet Grandad Ray didn't say anything. After his initial ribald glee over disturbing 'the young lovers' as he called them, he let his black mood roll over him once again. He gave up speaking to Winnie and Simon altogether.

Simon watched him going about his business – from garage to living room and out to the pub – and he waited for the inevitable storm to break. Grandad would burst out eventually, he was sure. He would accuse his grandson of theft. His own grandson – whom he'd taken in and given shelter and food. Simon had betrayed him. And the worst thing about it was that it was all true.

On Friday night Simon's phone bleeped and Kelly had sent a message:

Terrance is taking some convincing. I've explained what we need the cash for. He is thinking about it.

Simon smiled. He liked the way Kelly never abbreviated herself when she wrote texts. She spelled out each word laboriously.

'What's this?' Winnie said, watching him over the top of her novel. 'Is this your Kelly, hm?' She looked at him indulgently. 'What are you two cooking up?'

'Nothing,' he said quickly. He didn't want to tell Gran anything yet. Just in case the excursion didn't happen. Next Friday. A whole week away. This time next week the literary lunch would be over and done with . . . He just had to make sure they could get there. But he didn't like the sound of what Kelly was saying. She was having to convince Terrance. The Exchange owner didn't believe that the magazines they had stolen were worth the price they wanted.

But they had to be! After everything they'd gone through to get them out of the house! After betraying his grandad and all.

As if on cue his grandad returned home at that point. He surveyed the living room blearily and grunted at the sight of Winnie and Simon, both holding novels, both under the glare of their reading lamps.

'Can I get you a ham sandwich?' asked Winnie, jumping up. 'Do you want your cocoa, Ray?'

'No,' he said, crossing the room.

'I've made some broth,' she said. 'I could warm it up . . .'

'I don't want anything,' he said, and then he was gone.

Winnie sighed and gave a fake little laugh as she sat back in her armchair. 'He's off to that garage of his again.'

Simon nodded, filled with dread. Surely his grandad had realised by now that his magazines were gone. When would he say something? What would he do?

It was bright and freezing the next morning. Simon and his gran were togged up in scarves and hats and umpteen layers as they queued for the bus. Winnie was fussing over some metal contraptions she had bought to go over the soles of her boots, to prevent her slipping on the ice. They were digging into her feet, she claimed.

They hadn't seen anything of Ray that morning, but that wasn't unusual on a Saturday. He always slept in, revelling in the undisturbed quiet of the bungalow on the day that Winnie and Simon took their trip on the bus.

'Can you feel it in the air?' she asked Simon, as the bus wound through the industrial estate outside Kelly's town. 'It's all Christmassy. All of a sudden. It happens overnight. A different night each year.' She grinned at him. 'I woke up feeling all special.'

He shrugged. 'I'm not sure.' He was thinking about his own surprises. He'd had a text from Kelly at nine o'clock that morning. It was oddly but thrillingly concise: Success!

She had convinced Terrance to pay up. So they were going to do it. They were going to do this for his gran. It was going to work.

Even without knowing of their plans, Winnie seemed buoyant and excited this morning. She claimed it was because she felt Christmassy (oh – he didn't want to think about *that* yet), but he realised it was really because she'd be seeing Terrance in the Exchange. His gran was just about quivering with anticipation, clutching her shopping bag on the back seat of the bus.

'You really like him, don't you?' Simon asked her.

'Hm?' She looked sideways at him, and realised who he

meant. 'Oh, now,' she said. 'Don't go getting any silly ideas. He's just a very nice friend. A proper old-fashioned gentleman.'

'Kelly reckons he fancies you.' Simon couldn't resist mixing things.

Winnie's eyes flashed and then crinkled up with unalloyed pleasure. 'Oh!' she said. 'I can't say that anyone's *fancied* me in about forty years! Fancy? Me! That's ridiculous.'

'Not impossible, though,' said Simon. 'You've kept yourself smart. You're still . . . pretty.'

His gran was blushing, with two high spots of hot pink on her cheeks. 'Well. I make an effort to look as nice as I can. Not like some of these old ladies. But really, Simon. I'm an old married woman . . . I've told you before. I'm past all of that.' She mouthed the word 'that' very primly, as if it was the safest way to allude to a whole world of sensual temptations.

'Rubbish,' Simon laughed. 'Terrance obviously doesn't think so. He's not past it, either.'

'But he's not got any arms!' Winnie cried, starting to laugh. 'I mean, what can you do with a man with no arms?'

Simon was amazed at her being so candid. 'So you've thought about it!' he accused.

Immediately his gran clammed up. She looked ashamed.

217

'Indeed I haven't,' she told him, and looked away, at the shabby houses and shops of the South Road, until they arrived at the stop closest to the Book Exchange.

Once inside, as the consoling amber gloom settled around them, Simon watched his gran hold a whispered conversation with Terrance. Then Kelly slid up to him and stood at his elbow. She was like a spy at a rendezvous. She was loving the drama of all of this. She kissed him lightly on the cheek.

'I've got them,' she said.

'What?'

'These.' She pushed three cardboard tickets into his hand. He grinned at her, knowing he didn't have to look to see what they were. 'Well done, Kelly.'

She shrugged nonchalantly. 'I had to talk him into it. He gave me the exact amount. I told him what we were doing. Well, look how he's behaving around her. He's so in love with her. He'd do anything to make her happy.'

Simon gulped. In love with her? He narrowed his eyes, watching Terrance walking Winnie along a wall of bookcases, sliding a particular volume out for her – expertly, with his stiff arms.

'Have you told her yet?' asked Kelly. 'Have you told her what we're taking her to?'

Exchange

Kelly was more excited about it than Simon was. 'Not yet,' he said. 'I wanted to wait till it was definite. I didn't want to raise her hopes.'

He told her that afternoon. After they had managed to drag themselves away from the Exchange and say their goodbyes to Kelly and Terrance.

'See you on Friday, sunshine,' Kelly hissed, touching his nose.

'Sssh.'

Winnie and Simon shared a pot of tea in a nearby cafe and that was when he told his gran about the literary lunch. He produced the tickets and laid them out. They were cream and embossed with gold: special as wedding invitations.

Winnie was amazed and horrified.

'Where did you get the money . . .?'

'Never mind that,' Simon said firmly.

Winnie narrowed her eyes.

'Really,' he said. 'Don't worry about the money. It's all sorted out.'

'But . . .' she gasped. 'But . . .'

Simon laughed at her gawping expression. All around them the cafe was going about its everyday business. Steam was billowing out of the cappuccino machine; the waitress

219

was noisily knocking coffee grounds into the bin. Latin dance music was vibrating through the wooden floors.

'Ada Jones,' said Winnie, shaking her head. 'After all this time . . .'

'We're going to have a brilliant afternoon. The lunch menu is on the back of the tickets. It sounds gorgeous . . .' Suddenly he was keen to stress the other aspects of the event next Friday: not just the reunion-with-Ada part. Just in case that didn't work out. He didn't want that to be the be-all and end-all of their day out.

'Simon . . .' said Winnie. 'This is so thoughtful of you. I can't believe . . .' Her voice trailed away. Then she turned the colour of raspberry mousse. 'Oh, but she wouldn't want to see me again, would she? Just imagine . . . how awful it would be, if she doesn't even remember me?'

Simon moved to say something, but his gran was in a world of her own, roving over the possibilities. 'Oh no, Ada has left all her poverty-stricken past life behind her, hasn't she? Right behind her. She's grand. She's a famous lady now. What would she think? Her shameful past coming back to haunt her . . .' Winnie fell quiet. Then she looked at Simon and giggled. 'Thank you, Simon. It's a *delicious* idea.'

*

Coming home that teatime in the early dark, Simon found that he was starting to feel Christmassy after all. It was hard to put into words. A rising sense of excitement, of optimism. A feeling that, if he could just get past these last few weeks of school, his ongoing sense of dread would dissipate: he could relax.

All the way home he looked out of the black, shiny windows of the bus and counted Christmas trees in front rooms and felt a bit childish for doing it. It was what he had always done – in the back seat of his parents' car as a kid. His mum had started him on the game – the running tally of Christmas trees – when they used to drive forty miles up the motorway to visit his grandparents.

Winnie was reading out the menu on the back of the lunch tickets. 'Look at all the choices,' she said. 'Melon balls or Scottish salmon. And look at the trimmings for the main course . . . Oh, and the desserts . . .!' Then she looked at him sharply. 'Is Terrance coming along?'

Simon shook his head. 'I didn't think to invite him . . .'

Winnie dismissed the thought. 'There's no reason why he should. I'm just being silly.'

Simon hesitated. Part of him wanted to tell her how the Exchange owner had helped to make the trip possible, but he couldn't do that.

'What will I wear?' she said. 'Shall I splash out on something new? I'll have to make a hair appointment. Rini will be booked solid with all the old ladies and their old folks' parties . . .'

Winnie spent the rest of the bus journey fretting happily like this.

Their buoyant mood lasted until they got off the bus, walked across town and reached the end of their street.

'I can smell something funny,' Winnie said, instantly alert.

'Me too,' said Simon, sniffing.

It was an almost homely smell, like woodsmoke. Like there would be a blazing hearth to welcome them home. Except that the bungalow only had a gas fire and radiators. And the blaze was in the back garden. It was dying down now, unattended, smouldering orange and sending out plumes of choking violet smoke.

It was burning paper.

Winnie and Simon hurried into the garden, wafting the dark, crackling air with their arms, staring appalled at the mass of blackened paperbacks and the glowing cinders that Grandad had left for them to see.

'No,' Simon whispered. 'He wouldn't.'

Motes and smuts were still alight and floating around their heads, trying to land in their hair and on their clothes.

Winnie stopped brushing them away as she stood there, dumbfounded at the sight of her books. They could see half-scorched pages with some type still legible amongst the ashes. Lurid paperback covers were curled and blackened and they, too, were being eaten up in the last of the blaze.

'Ray!' Winnie threw back her head and howled up into the smoke-darkened sky. 'Ray!'

They found him lying in the bed he shared with Winnie. All the white pillows and duvet and tangled sheets were blackened with soot that he'd dragged in on his clothes and shoes. He lay there shivering and coughing in his dirt. Simon took in the scene in a moment – noting the empty lager can on his bedside table, just as he had noticed the others in the living room and kitchen; just as he'd noticed the ransacked, depleted bookshelves.

Winnie had become very calm and grim, Simon realised. He would have preferred it if she was furious and shrieking. His gran clenched her fists and glared coldly at Grandad in the bed. Grandad Ray was aware of their presence, even as he was wracked with another coughing fit; doubling up with it. His face, all filthy like that, was almost comical.

'You stupid, stupid old man,' Winnie said quickly. 'What have you done?'

Ray fell back flat on the mattress, wheezing heavily, as if the sheer force of Winnie's stare was exhausting to him.

'I haven't burned them all,' he said feebly. 'Just . . .'

'You've burned enough,' Winnie said. 'You've burned plenty. You stupid, stupid old man. Everything stinks. Everything is spoiled.'

'I didn't burn them all,' he protested.

'It's enough,' she said.

'The fire got out of hand. I breathed in too much smoke. I had to come indoors and lie down. I'm sorry.' He gasped. Simon flinched at the bubbling, choking noise in his chest. It sounded like a saucepan kept too long on the boil.

'You could have killed yourself,' said Winnie. 'Messing about like that, drunk. You could have burned the whole place down. Do you realise that? We'd have had nothing then, do you hear me? Nothing!' Then her suppressed fury finally broke and she was shaking with grief. 'You could have gone and killed yourself,' she sobbed. 'You stupid, stupid old man.'

Fifteen

She sighed and took a very dainty sip of sherry. She was on to her third 'medicinal' sweet sherry by now, as she and Simon sat talking late into the night. 'All I had, my only consolation . . . my one bit of freedom . . . was my books. And he knew that. He even envied them. He did! He resented the time I was off in my own world. And so he had to destroy them, didn't he? He had to take that life of mine and set a light to it. Watch it go up in flames . . .'

The smoke had wreathed itself through all the rooms of their home. It would be weeks before they would be rid of the acrid, heavy scent of scorched paper. It was in Simon's clothes and his hair. As he sat listening to his gran and watching her upend the sherry glass into her mouth, he was conscious of the gaps on the bookshelves around them, and the one or two dropped books lying on the carpet. He had already checked out his own room and found that maybe a third of his own collection had gone. His grandad had grabbed up armloads, it seemed, quite randomly, with indiscriminate spite – and lugged them outside to feed the flames.

Simon felt quite nonplussed at losing his books like this. It didn't touch him as it might have done. He didn't know why he felt so numb about it.

Why had Grandad Ray done it? What had tipped him over into this extreme behaviour? It was brutal of him. Savage. It was the kind of thing that a desperate, drunk, lonely man would do. Out of revenge.

Grandad Ray had found his magazines were missing, Simon realised. And he'd known that either Simon or Winnie had stolen them. And this is what he'd done in response.

'All I had were my books,' Gran was saying. 'My only consolation.' Suddenly she looked up guiltily at her grandson. 'No, that's not true. You're my consolation, too, Simon. Just like your mother was.' She set down her slender glass and blew her nose very noisily. 'Now she's gone, and so have my books.' Winnie smiled wearily. 'But I've still got you, haven't I, lovely? I've still got you.'

Simon felt awkward. He grinned and nodded but actually he was beginning to feel like he was looking at Winnie down the wrong end of a telescope. She seemed distant and dim and indistinct. He was tired and overwrought, but with a sudden clarity of thought he realised that he was feeling further and further away from his grandparents and their world. Their decades-long squabbles and their petty behaviour and even acts as extreme as the burning of books – it all seemed remote to him.

He needed to get away from them. Soon. He would need to escape from their lives. He had no idea how he would do this, or where he might go.

Kelly? Maybe she represented some possibility to him. The idea of escape? Of a proper, adult life – beyond the confines of his grandparents' stymied relationship and their small, stuffy, now sooty bungalow.

Would he run away somewhere to be with Kelly? Could that really happen?

He looked at the carriage clock on the mantelpiece. It was after one in the morning. His gran had dozed off in her chair.

No, he thought. His mind was suddenly very clear. He wouldn't run off anywhere with Kelly. He wanted to feel that being with her was right. He would love for it to be like that. But it wasn't, quite. He knew that now.

He shook his gran gently awake.

'Winnie . . .?'

She roused herself, wiping sherry from her lips with her cardigan sleeve. 'Look at me. I'm like a blumming bag lady.'

'Where will you sleep?'

She scowled. 'Not with him. He's got all the sheets black.' She shrugged. 'I'll bed down on the settee,' she said. 'If you'll fetch me a blanket.'

'OK,' Simon said.

During the next week Grandad had to stay in bed, chastened and coughing. Meekly he submitted to his wife's gruff care. He wouldn't go to hospital to have his chest checked out. He was an old, old smoker, he said. He didn't want them looking at his lungs. They'd be full of crackling twigs and dead leaves and tar. The doctor came round and listened to his back through a stethoscope and looked down his throat and asked Winnie terse questions, and she shrugged and replied non-committally.

This was an old married couple, Simon thought. Just going about the routinised business of caring for each other; of tending after each other in sickness and old age. His gran simply had to forget about her sacrificed novels, if she wanted to go on living under the same roof as the old man. You could go mad bearing grudges, she told Simon. You just had to let these things go, in the end.

She didn't say much to Grandad, though. She cleaned and fed him while he lay recuperating in their bed – which was a startling white again. Winnie went quiet and didn't even talk to Simon that much.

'You still want to go, don't you?' he asked her, that Monday in the kitchen.

'Hm?' She was dozy in the daytime. She hadn't been sleeping too well on the sofa.

'You still want to go on Friday,' he said, '. . . to the Literary Lunch . . .?'

'Of course I do,' she gasped. 'What do you think . . .? Why would I change my mind?'

He didn't know.

The next day he came home from school to find Winnie on her knees in the black smudgy mud of the back garden. She was picking through the nasty debris of the fire. She looked up at him, almost shame-faced. 'I'm checking to see if I can rescue anything,' she said. 'Look.' She pointed to a heap of charred remnants.

'Leave them,' he said. 'We can always buy more . . .'

'Buy more!' she cried out, struggling to her feet. 'Buy more, indeed! Now, there's the voice of spoiled youth. We used to have to make do and mend. We had to look after things. We couldn't just go out and . . . buy more!' She

229

picked up the four or five cindery artefacts she had salvaged and realised they were beyond rescue. She sighed and threw them back onto the ashes.

'I think they've driven each other round the bend,' Simon told Kelly on the phone that night. 'All that resentment and claustrophobia. They've both gone crackers.'

'It sounds awful,' Kelly said. She was concerned, but refused to feel guilty about events at the bungalow. She didn't think Grandad Ray had done what he'd done because they had stolen his mags. 'That old devil is a powder keg,' she said. 'Moods up and down like that. He's bound to do daft things. It's just lucky that no one was hurt.'

'Hm,' said Simon. He was in the phone box in the town centre, amazed that it had been fixed. His mobile had run out of credit and he couldn't have spoken so freely on the phone at home. It was dark now and he was only meant to be out buying milk at the grocery. He was tapping his twenty pence pieces together when he realised that the kids who hung around the phone box at night were returning to their habitual post. He could see them crossing over from their favoured off-licence – Booze 'N' Cigs 'N' Papers – bringing their cheap fags and cider with them. The oldest boy was in a T-shirt that showed off his muscles.

'Damn,' Simon said softly.

'I'm going to tell Terrance what's going on,' Kelly was saying. 'You know how he feels about Winnie. We both do.'

'What are you saying?' Simon found it hard to concentrate, watching the hard kids approach. He had a sudden vision of himself trapped inside the phone box. But it was OK. If he could just finish this conversation with Kelly, he could make a dash for home. He didn't want to get into some scene with these kids tonight.

'Terrance really cares for her, Simon,' Kelly was saying earnestly. 'He's actually started to confide in me. I've never heard him talk like that about anyone. He usually keeps things so close to his chest. He's not been close to anyone since he lost his family. That was a fire, too, you know. Lost them all. Two kids. Both under five. And his wife. They all went up in a fire in the first bookshop he owned, years ago . . .'

'When did he tell you this?' Kelly's timing was terrible. He really wanted to hear the rest of her story, but as he stared through the scratched, graffitied glass of the call box, he could see that he'd been rumbled. His cider-swigging Nemeses had clocked him making use of their telephone.

'Like I say: he's been opening up to me lately. Telling me stuff. And it's all down to Winnie, Simon. I really think he's in love with her . . .'

'Er, Kelly,' Simon said. 'Really, I've got to go now.' With no further ado he dropped the receiver and slammed out of the phone box. To the astonishment of the kids who hung around that spot each night, he came hurtling through them like a bat out of hell.

'Simon? Simon?' Kelly was still shouting. Her voice came out of the dangling receiver, tinny and distorted.

The oldest lad picked it up. 'Hello?' he said.

'That's how he burned his arms,' Kelly said, thinking she had Simon's attention again. 'Going back to drag his kids out of the flames. Imagine. He must have held on and held on to them until . . . until . . .'

The kid in the phone box put the receiver down with a bang. He didn't know what she was on about.

Sixteen

Grandad Ray was just going to have to look after himself.

He had been waited on, hand and foot, all week. Spending Friday alone in the bungalow wouldn't hurt him one bit.

'I don't understand, though,' he said. 'Where are you both going to?' He looked flummoxed, peeping over the bedspread as Winnie dressed in the corner of their room. She was reaching into the heavy old wardrobe and picking out her very best, pale cream suit. It had pink piping and a neat little hat. It was her wedding suit, really, but it was many years since Winnie and Ray had attended such an event.

Winnie looked at Ray, and for a second – just a second – her heart went out to him.

He looked helpless, there in the bed where he'd lain for a full week, coughing and spluttering and hoping she'd forgive him. He still looked a little singed around the edges, but she knew that must be her imagination. She reached into the wardrobe for her best blouse. All those ruffles at the front could do with an iron.

'Where are you going?' Ray said weakly. 'Somewhere posh?'

She forced herself to shrug and to look away from his imploring eyes. 'It's nothing to do with you.'

'You'd . . . You'd not be going out with some other fella, would you?' he asked. 'I mean, you'd tell me if you were going to leave me, wouldn't you?'

Winnie struggled to keep her voice steady, startled as she was by his question. 'No, I'm not going out to see some other fella,' she laughed. 'Who'd have me? It's you who's had the best years of my life, you silly old fool.'

It was just before nine on Friday morning. There was a pleasurable, rising tension about the place; a tingling anxiety that the old man couldn't help but notice.

'I haven't heard Simon leave for school,' he said. 'He hasn't popped his head in here, to say goodbye.'

Winnie thought about Simon, pressing his favourite shirt in the kitchen, his hair all slick with wax. He would be her perfect gentlemanly companion today. He looked so handsome and grown-up. Winnie would be so proud to introduce him to Ada. This is my grown-up grandson, Ada. That was

234

something Ada didn't have – as far as Winnie knew. No kids, no grandchildren. That was something where Winnie beat her hands down.

'Simon's not going to school today, Ray.'

'What? What's going on? You're letting him skive off . . .?'

'He's told me that nothing very important is happening at his school today. Where he's going with me today – that's more important.'

'And you really won't tell me where that is?'

'No,' she said, folding her outfit over her arm and preparing to leave him. 'Like I say. It hasn't got anything to do with you, Ray.'

As she left him, closed the door and scooted through the hallway towards the kitchen, Winnie was marvelling at herself; at the way she had handled Ray. Since his efforts at destroying all her books – and her nerves, and her happiness – last Saturday, the one thing that she had firmly resolved was that she wouldn't let him upset her again. She wouldn't let him touch her. None of his niggling or needling, his fussing or bullying. She would deal with him lightly but firmly. It was the worst thing she could imagine doing to him: never to take him seriously again.

The postman was standing in the kitchen. Simon, shirtless, concentrating, was signing for the parcel which lay, invitingly, on the table. It would be that Kelly again, sending him things. Vaguely Winnie hoped that Simon was recipro-cating and that he wasn't just taking off her.

The sight of her grandson's pale, bare shoulders surprised her. She hadn't seen his bare chest like this since he was a proper little boy, years ago. Now the sprouting hairs around his nipples and across his chest alarmed her. He's a man, she thought. Of course, he's a man already. Absurdly, she thought about chewy crusts of toast and telling him to eat them up so they'd put hairs on his chest. So he had grown up properly and it was partly down to her. He had grown up kind and thoughtful, too, and today he was treating her. She would dress up in her finest outfit and they would have a wonderful day together.

The postman nodded and said good morning. He left as she checked that the iron was still hot. 'Another present from Kelly?'

'It's for you,' he said.

She hurried over. The label was written out extremely tidily. Unnaturally tidily, really. As if someone had to take extreme care to make it legible.

'Heavy,' Simon said. 'It feels like—'

'Books,' Winnie sighed happily, once – a matter of

seconds later – she had ripped off the brown paper and opened the box. 'Terrance,' she said, though at first she couldn't find a note inside. She knew it was him. This box exuded that spicy scent of the Exchange, and it was crammed with fifteen thick, worn paperbacks. They were Ada Jones's first fifteen novels: fat, yellow, second-hand and familiar. She let her fingers walk across their ridged spines. In the first page of the first novel she discovered a short message from the owner of the Exchange, written in that distinctive, extra-neat hand.

'He says he heard about our . . . disaster,' Winnie told Simon. 'He wanted to do something. He wanted to give me these novels.'

'That's lovely,' Simon said, suddenly conscious of being half naked in the kitchenette. He slipped his warm, green paisley shirt on. 'Kelly must have told him what's been happening here.'

Winnie went on, 'He also says he was furious that my husband could ever do such a thing. He can't believe that I'm not . . . cherished and protected. He says that's what I deserve . . .'

'He put all that?' asked Simon, surprised.

Winnie nodded. She slipped the books back into place in the cardboard box, where they fitted snugly into chronological order. 'Let's take this with us. Let's ask Ada if she will sign them all for me.'

'I'd better ring for a taxi,' Simon said. 'We don't want to get a bus. We want to arrive in style . . .'

Winnie agreed distantly (usually she would have questioned the expense). 'He signed his note with all his love, Simon,' she said. 'What do you think of that?'

Simon swallowed. 'I don't know.'

Winnie frowned. 'I'm amazed he can write at all, with those two plastic hands of his. Let alone so neatly. He's amazing, really, isn't he?'

The route to Kelly's town seemed different. All the landmarks – the fields and the buildings and the long streets of shops – looked quite different when you were sitting low down in a car, and not up on the back seat of a bus. It felt luxurious, sliding through the streets like this, skimming along the frosty roads, in the cramped, cosy plush of the taxi.

First they picked Kelly up at the flats where she lived with her dad. She was standing waiting in her latest Goth ensemble. 'Something to frighten the old ladies,' she'd joked on the phone. But actually, in her scarlet and black lace and velveteen, she looked puckish and punkish, like a strange kind of fairy.

'You got your parcel, then,' she said to Winnie as she slid into the car.

'He's very kind.'

'He's smitten.'

'Oh, hush.'

'Smitten' seemed like a very old-fashioned word in Kelly's mouth, Simon thought. It was an Ada Jones-type word.

'Are we all excited?' Kelly grinned.

Winnie nodded quickly. 'A bit nervous. I'm not sure what to expect from one of these do's . . .'

'Just enjoy it,' said Kelly.

It wasn't quite midday yet, but the sky was turning dark, woolly, congested and grey – as if it was deciding whether to rain or snow. But the temperature was dropping, severely. They could feel that, even inside the taxi. When they stepped out, right outside the King's Arms Hotel in the centre of the town, the air seemed to tingle and shimmer with frost.

Winnie, sighing and clasping her matching bag and box of books, gazed up at the impressively wedding cake-like frontage of the old hotel. Simon paid the taxi and watched it speed off. Kelly nudged him. 'You look very nice, too, sunshine. You've scrubbed up well.'

'Erm,' said Winnie. 'One of you will have to go in first. I'm a bit shy of places like this . . .'

They swirled in through the revolving doors, disoriented and warmed, once inside, by the sight of scarlet furnishings, draperies, gleaming brass fittings and chandeliers. Everything was soft: the lighting, the music tinkling away, just out of hearing, and the luscious pile of the carpet as they shuffled across the foyer. Other people were gathering here too. They were having morning tea in the high-backed leather armchairs, half obscured by the potted palms, watching each new arrival with unconcealed interest. Lots of them were Winnie's own age, dressed up to the nines in similar fashion. Kelly's slick boots and studded belt raised a few eyebrows.

Not from the concierge, though, who took their gold and white tickets and smiled warmly at the three of them, directing them to the Rainbow Function Room, on the third floor.

The dining room was much larger and busier than they had expected. The Rainbow Room had about thirty large tables laid out in a square. At the far end, one table was up on a tall podium. 'High table,' Winnie murmured, nodding and pointing. For the guest of honour. Now, where were they supposed to go? There were seat numbers on their tickets. She hoped they wouldn't be put next to anyone awful. There was always that chance, even at a do as smart as this. You never knew who you'd end up rubbing shoulders with . . . Winnie was gabbling happily away as they slid between tables and brushed past other, well-dressed Ada fans. She's gabbling because she's happy, Simon thought. She's letting her mouth run away with her because she's so excited.

'Oh, look at these beautiful centrepieces, Simon,' she was saying. 'Lilies and irises and whatnot. They must have spent thousands on the flowers alone . . . And look! This is proper, heavy silver, this.' She picked up a knife and found the place setting with her own name on it. 'Lovely penmanship,' she said approvingly.

The candles were lit and their small white flames bobbed gently, bathing them all in a flattering light as they scraped back their chairs and sat down. Already the room was mostly filled. Simon and Kelly were fairly unsurprised to find that they were the only young people there. The air was thick with old lady scents: violets and lilac and rose.

Waiters and waitresses were flitting about, tending to everyone's wants. They were coming round first of all with frosted, pale green decanters of wine. 'I could get to like this treatment,' Winnie said.

They had time, as they settled, to examine the other people at their table. A very broad-faced, well-spoken woman called Marcia took control of the situation, and made everyone at their table introduce themselves to each other. Simon thought that this was a good idea, but he could see that Winnie wasn't at all impressed with Marcia pushing herself forward. The woman had a plainly dyed magenta bouffant and was wearing dark glasses indoors.

'I feel like I have been reading Ada Jones all my life,' she was declaring to the table at large, as the waiter came to take their orders. 'I was very young when she started publishing her novels, and I have read each and every one, annually, as they have been published. I must say, I prefer her earlier ones, all about her awful, squalid background in the slums. They're more authentic, somehow. But I won't read a book by anyone else at all.'

'No one?' asked Kelly, aghast. 'No one at all?'

'Why should I?' Marcia grinned ferociously. 'All I need to know about the world is to be found in the novels of Ada Jones. All human life is there, as they say. I really think the woman is a genius.'

Winnie was pursing her lips, Simon noticed. No, she wasn't impressed with Marcia at all. Nor with her mousey friend Karen, either, who – it turned out – hadn't read a single Ada Jones novel in all her life. She was just here for the lunch, the company and the afternoon out.

'Some people have got more money than sense,' Winnie

whispered to Simon, over the rising, aviary-like noise of the ladies as their starters arrived.

'So where is Ada?' asked Simon. Their wide plates of colourful antipasti were being set before them. He toyed with slivers of Parma ham and chilled melon and all the while he was peering about with great interest. People from a bookshop were setting up a stall by the main entrance. They had put what seemed to be a golden throne by the signing table, where they were unloading heavy stacks of brand new, brick-thick paperbacks. (Winnie's box of books was under their table. 'Shall I look after that for you, madam?' the waiter had asked. 'No!' Winnie burst out.)

Simon scanned the high table, where some grand and confident-looking people were now sitting – eating and chuckling and chatting away. Who were they? Book trade people, publishers, booksellers, close personal friends of the author? All in a line, surveying this extensive crowd, tucking in happily to their Literary Lunch. But where was Ada herself? Simon squinted along the row of nodding, chomping, talking heads at the high table.

'Have you seen her yet?' Kelly asked, pointing into the air with a forkful of melon ball.

'Where?' Winnie gasped.

They all saw Ada at the same moment. She was right in

the middle of that exalted rank on the podium, but she was so tiny that her head hardly poked up over the table. She was talking to a huge bear of a man on her left, and he made her seem even more diminutive. Her hair was white and hanging down loose. It looked very soft in the candlelight. She was laughing as they watched her, and sipping on a tumbler of what must have been water. She didn't touch her dinner at all.

'That's her,' said Simon. 'That's really her.'

Even as she talked to her fellow diners at the high table, Ada's keen, intelligent eyes were observing the roomful of people who had come to bask in her presence.

'Don't you just want to go over there?' Kelly whispered to Winnie. 'You've got more right to talk to her than any of that lot.'

Simon was thinking along similar lines. The old Winnie and Ada, all those years ago, wouldn't have sat like this, so near and so far apart, unable to talk to each other. A thought struck Simon: would Ada have noticed Winnie's presence already? He could see how Ada was taking in every detail of the well-heeled crowd. Her eyes – all heavy mascara and silver (silver!) eyeshadow – were flicking around the room as the delicious main course was served.

'You can see it's still her,' Winnie said. 'She's still pale and skinny. She's got that same slightly bent nose. She used to say her dad had hit her.' Even though she was in a smart, dark, quite obviously expensive trouser suit, it was plain to Winnie, at least, where Ada had come from. The dirty house next door. The rough family that the whole street was ashamed of.

The air was all clattering silver and clinking crystal, and the scents of stuffing and bread sauce and molten, glistening vegetables. Across the Rainbow Room, shrieks of delight were going up as the first few bangs went off. 'They're pulling crackers!' Winnie said, scandalised. Simon was surprised, too. He had expected a Literary Lunch to be a more solemn, intellectual affair.

Then Kelly and Simon and Marcia and Karen and the rest of their table were brandishing crackers and making Winnie join in and soon everyone in the room was wearing tissue paper party hats.

These hats stayed on, too – some of them at a more jaunty angle – through the rich, heavy puddings, the red wine, the dessert wine, the sherry afterwards. After all of this, everyone sat back and suddenly an unobtrusive little man was standing up on the podium and making them applaud the kitchen staff and the waiting staff, and then he was giving a long, rambling speech, full of praise for Ada Jones.

'That unassuming local lass who left the region so long ago, to make her own particular mark on the much wider world out there . . .' There was a ripple of polite amusement then: Ada was scowling in open contempt at his words. Her readers – used to her sense of humour; her impatience with snobs and buffoons – lapped up every ironic twitch of her eyebrows. The hotel manager grew flustered and raced to the end of his toadying speech and, at last, to thunderous applause, left the floor open for Ada Jones.

She didn't move very far. She simply stood up, in front of her chair. She didn't do anything to grab their attention at all. She placed her hands on the tablecloth in front of her and leaned forward slightly, as if at a lectern. She was smiling and glancing at every table in turn. They had miked her up and so her wheezing breath came issuing out of the loudspeakers set into the walls at discreet intervals. She was gathering up her breath and it was obvious that there was something not quite right with her lungs. Her chest sounded like a clock that had been wound up too tight: all the cogs and springs were clicking and cracking and longing to chime. Ada coughed – too close to the microphone – and the sound boomed and bounced around the room. She covered her mouth with her hand and raised the glass tumbler to her lips.

Simon noticed that, in her wispy, white hair, she was

wearing a single, girlish clip, to keep it out of her face, and that touched him, for some reason. It was as if Ada had never changed her hairstyle since she was a little girl.

'I am amazed,' Ada began. 'I'm amazed to see so many of you here.' They all jumped at the sound of her voice. After all her wheezing they had expected a very small, whispering voice, conserving her air. But Ada had the loudest, most booming voice they had ever heard. Only Winnie was smiling in recognition.

'I've never really given readings on my home turf,' Ada said. 'I didn't think anyone would come out to see me. It's fantastically difficult to imagine, when you get to my state of ancientness and decrepitude, to imagine anyone wanting to see you at all . . .'

Simon looked along the table and saw that his gran was staring at Ada, and she looked pleased, perplexed and disturbed all at the same time. Others, too, were alarmed at how unwell Ada seemed to be. Kelly had told Simon that this was likely to be the last public appearance that Ada was determined to make, but he hadn't absorbed the truth of that. Here, though, Ada looked a lot more ill than anyone had expected. Simon thought Ada looked a great deal older than his gran.

When Ada picked up the new hardback to read from, the

thick, luridly colourful novel seemed almost too heavy for her. The bear-like man beside Ada inched forward and, for a moment, it seemed that he was going to hold the book up for her, in front of her nose.

Her tiny hands were chapped and red. Her skin seemed so thin that her nerves and veins were almost visible, pulsing away inside of her.

Ada read in a strong, forthright voice. Her accent crept back as she lost herself in her own story, and took all of her sated, tipsy, party-hatted audience with her. Back, back into the past. The new novel returned her to the location of her very first book; to the setting of her youth. Simon's heart beat faster and his temples pounded with booze fumes and sadness as he realised that Ada was revisiting the old streets and houses, and revelling in the tarry, salty scents of the coastline, and the cawing of the gulls, and of mammies shouting on doorsteps for the kids to come home as night fell.

Ada read for almost an hour, wracked with coughing fits, asking her large companion to refill her glass now and then with her 'special water' (laughter then – he filled it with Russian vodka and bottled tonic water that he pulled out of a carrier bag kept under the table). But even with all these distractions the spell didn't break. Ada held their attention and their imagination and kept them all trapped in that past. For that afternoon, everyone – Simon, Kelly, Winnie, the ladies, the wine waiters and booksellers – they were all playing out at teatime, some time in the middle of the last century: playing in the wrong places, down by the sand dunes and the docks, with a gang of rough girls. For her last novel Ada had returned them all to the very beginning.

When she finished Simon realised that everyone else was applauding rowdily, happily, and they were all getting up, to leave their places at table, to get into the queue to buy the new book and have it personally signed. Simon was still in a daze, still back there running wild in the past, with scabby knees and unwashed hair. He turned to see that his gran had tears running down her face, making runnels through the powder.

'I'm making a show of myself,' she gasped, when Simon tapped her arm.

'Let's go and meet her,' he smiled.

It turned out that everyone who had eaten lunch and listened to Ada read wanted to buy the new hardback. 'No wonder she's a bestseller,' Kelly said. 'They're grabbing them up, look.'

Winnie, Kelly and Simon got into place, near the very

back of the queue. Others, more used to the form at these events, had dashed into position almost as soon as Ada had closed her book.

'Wasn't she wonderful?' Simon grinned. 'It was great, wasn't it? Hearing it in her actual voice. It was like being back there . . .' He looked at his gran, who was beaming, tight-lipped. She looked pleased and proud, he thought. As if Ada was her protégée – which, he thought, she was, in a way. 'Her new novel sounds good, doesn't it?' Simon asked her.

Winnie nodded firmly.

'You've got to get a copy . . .'

She shook her head. 'I never buy hardbacks. Twenty pounds! I can wait for the paperback. That'll do for me.'

Simon was amazed. 'But . . . it's about . . . your home, again. She's gone back to your childhood again. You have to have it now . . .'

His gran gave him a complacent smile. 'I can wait. I've waited this long, haven't I? To go back to the beginning. I think I can wait a bit more.'

'Have you heard this?' Simon turned to Kelly. 'She won't buy the book. They'll chuck her out of the queue . . .'

Kelly smiled and shrugged. She was carrying the box of books sent by Terrance.

'I'll wait,' Winnie said again. 'Maybe I'll wait until it comes into the Exchange.'

There was a bit of a fracas with one of the booksellers – a very young and trendy woman – who claimed that they weren't allowed to get their *old* novels signed by Ms Jones. Ms Jones was on an exceedingly tight schedule and had no time to sign anyone's *old* books. All Ms Jones would be signing today were the pristine copies of her *new* book, plenty of which were available for sale.

Kelly wasn't to be browbeaten. 'Forget it, love,' she told the bookseller. 'We've paid forty quid each to be here. And Mrs Thompson here is a very old friend of Ms Jones. Probably her oldest friend in the world. So, if Mrs Thompson wanted her *bum* signing, never mind her old books, that's what would happen, OK?'

The young woman blanched. She wasn't used to dealing with Kelly's sort. Not at events like this. 'Anyway,' said Kelly, 'what's so wrong with old books, eh?'

The bookseller looked down at the box Kelly was carrying, and shuddered as if she, too – just like Grandad Ray – thought of old books as tiny little coffins, full of dust, dead ideas, germs and lice. But she stopped bothering Kelly, Winnie and Simon, and went off to sell more new books.

'I thought she was going to throw us out,' Winnie

sighed. 'That would have been something.' She grinned, and started to tell them the tale of how she and Ada had been chucked out of the Central Library, the first time they had visited it. How they'd been caught looking at pictures in medical books and giggling under the stone dome of the reference room, unaware that their giggles were being magnified, amplified and bounced around the whole building.

'She won't even know me now,' Winnie said nervously, as the queue inched forward and their ears were filled with chattering and squealing and a tense expectancy that felt exactly like queueing for Santa Claus's grotto in the old department stores. 'But I'll be able to tell her that I remember her. Even without all of her fame and success, I'd have known that tiny urchin anywhere.'

It took more than an hour for the queue to dwindle down and for the end to be in sight. It seemed that every reader there wanted to linger and have a proper conversation with Ada Jones; to make that personal, human connection. Simon suspected that all of them had read the same article as Kelly, and had learned that this would most likely be Ada's final public appearance.

As they came into view of her, they could see that her strength was flagging. She was a small figure hunched on

that ridiculous golden throne, her hands busy at work signing messages in the books. She seemed feeble but, Simon
realised, there was a great fortitude about her, too – as if all
that was keeping her going was sheer force of will.

That idea certainly fitted with the Ada his gran had
talked about and the Ada he was starting to know from her
novels.

The bumbling, bald, bear-like man was still standing at
Ada's right hand. He was there to open the books for her
and to keep her glass of 'special water' topped up. 'That must
be her husband,' Winnie said. 'The way she's bossing him
about like that. Eric, I think he's called. Very posh. But
look – he's got his shirt buttons fastened up wrong . . .' It
was true, there was a bulging flap of open shirt, displaying his
paunch to the queue of ladies. There was something affably
eccentric and blimpish about this Eric that Simon warmed
to. He could hear Ada's husband's fruity, slurred, cultivated
voice contributing to the various excitable greetings. He was
gently and subtly keeping the queue moving; keeping everyone happy.

At last it was their turn to come face to face with the doll-
like figure on the golden chair. Kelly slid the box of fifteen
books onto the table and started to pull them out, one at a
time. Simon was embarrassed by her determination. Ada

looked completely shattered by now. This close up, her complexion was waxen and her cheeks were sunken. But her eyes were blazing a brilliant green with interest.

Winnie had lost her nerve. To Simon's astonishment she started to pretend to be just any other punter.

'I hope you won't mind,' she said meekly. 'But I've brought a number of older books I'd like to have signed. I'm a very great fan, you see, and . . .'

Winnie kept her head down and all of the others were staring at her. Winnie blushed, aware of their attention. She pulled the lapels of her cream jacket together, fussily, over the ruffles of her best blouse and looked up, unsurely. Straight into the emerald green, sparkling, amused eyes of Ada Jones.

Ada laughed. 'How dare you stand there, pretending not to be you!' She cackled loudly and this turned quickly into a cough. Eric patted her back firmly till the coughs subsided. Ada narrowed her eyes. 'It is you, isn't it?'

Winnie looked surprised. 'What? You recognised me?' She turned on Simon and Kelly. 'You told her? You let her know I'd be here . . .?'

'No!' Simon laughed, protesting.

Ada wheezed and grinned, and wheezed some more. 'No, I recognised you for myself, you daft old witch. Of course I did! Sitting there like Lady Muck, all dolled up and looking down your snooty nose at everyone. Why, it had to be you.'

'Me! Looking down my nose!' cried Winnie.

'Yes! You always did! You always went on like you ruled the world.' Ada was on her feet now, somewhat unsteadily. Reaching out across the signing table with her red and purple-veined hands. 'Winnie,' she gasped. 'My God, woman, I've missed you.'

Simon and Kelly stood back then, as the two women embraced and sobbed loudly and clung to each other. Simon turned to look at Kelly, and all the amazed-looking booksellers and others still hanging about in the Rainbow Room, and now he could feel his own tears coming up to choke him.

Seventeen

Ray rolled over to the other side of the bed. To Winnie's side. He wasn't over this side very much. By late afternoon he was so bored that seeing how the world looked from this different vantage point seemed like an interesting thing to do. Next thing he knew, he was sitting up and going through the drawer in Winnie's bedside cabinet. This was sacrosanct. It was the kind of thing that Ray would never normally dream of doing.

But this was an emergency, really, wasn't it? His wife was out there somewhere, running around and getting up to who knew what. She was enjoying herself and couldn't even bring herself to tell him what she was doing. I'm going to lose her, Ray thought. After all these long years and the things – some of them terrible – that we've been through, I'm going to wind up losing her, even at this late stage.

He rummaged and ransacked and rifled through

Winnie's private things: the junk jewellery and hair clips and tickets and programmes and coins and souvenirs and keep-sakes. Beetling his brows and peering blearily, with no real clue what he was looking for, Ray examined it all. Her pass-port, sixteen years out of date. The photograph in the back looked like it was of another woman altogether.

He found notes. Silly little love notes scrawled on yel-lowing paper. He read them and his heart jumped up in justifiable ire, and a sudden blast of righteous jealousy. Until he realised that they were his own notes to Winnie. He recognised the handwriting, then the cantankerous, mock-ing tone. They hadn't really been love letters at all. They were about mundane things: reminders, lists. But she had kept them, all the same. She was a strange, old, secretive bird.

He found her membership card for that place, too. The Great Big Book Exchange. Ray fingered the small grey card thoughtfully, reading the address neatly printed on the back. That was the great, good place, wasn't it? The place where that Kelly worked. The shop that none of them could get enough of. They escaped there. They went to it like it was their sanctuary, like it was paradise. They went there to escape from this place; their lives; him.

Well. One day he'd just have to go there himself,

wouldn't he? And then he would see what all the fuss was about. Maybe then he would see the point.

He pulled on his slippers and eased himself out of bed, back onto his feet. He hadn't spent much time up and about this past week, and the effort of walking into the hall made him reel with dizziness. What he could do with was a drink. There'd be some cans left in the fridge.

He made his way there, turning the Book Exchange membership card round and round in his hand as he went.

Perhaps that's where they were today. They had dressed up for some special thing at that shop. Some kind of celebration. That's what it was.

Something that had nothing to do with him. Nothing to do with him at all.

Simon felt a bit like he did when he was bunking off school.

All the rules had changed. They had become reckless and spontaneous and they didn't know where they would end up next. He liked this feeling. Today it was like he and Kelly and his gran were a part of the in-crowd, sitting with Ada as she finished up business with the last of the literary-lunchers, and then with the booksellers and the hotel people.

Ada's husband Eric made sure they had some more sherry as the dining room was cleaned up around them and there came the echoing, clashing shouts and bangs of the debris being cleared away.

This was being behind the scenes. Ada – looking tired and drawn and like she would brook no arguments – had told them that they weren't to go shooting off anywhere. They weren't to disappear. She had said that Winnie and her grandson and his friend had to come home with her that very evening. Eric would be driving them: they had the car; he just needed to fetch it around to the front of the hotel. He would do so in just a minute, once they had finished up business. Ada really wanted Winnie to come back with her, to her house on the coast. It was only about ninety miles away, not far.

Winnie had, of course, been delighted. And fairly dumb-struck, too, Simon was amused to see. His gran had been dreading this reunion, in one way – in case it had all gone wrong, and Ada had rejected her. But this was all perfect. It seemed that Ada wanted them, really wanted them, to come and see her home. She was promising that Eric was a mar-vellous cook and host. He would look after them all. 'And I'm a fantastically sick old lady, so I don't have time or energy to beg you or cajole you,' Ada warned.

'You won't need to,' said Winnie firmly. She had her box of books (and Ada's new novel – gladly signed as a gift to her) on her lap. 'We'll just need to give my husband a ring . . .' When Ada turned to speak to her publicist, Winnie hissed at Simon: 'Would you talk to your grandad, Simon? I can't face it just now.'

Simon sighed. 'He probably won't even come to the phone.'

'Leave him a message then,' said Winnie, touching her hair. Would Ada think Winnie's perm a very old-ladyish style? Ada's own hair was hanging loose, mostly – unstyled, but not unbecoming. She gave the appearance of being above the thought of such things. Still though, when you examined Ada close to, you could see that she was wearing some very discreet and probably expensively tasteful jewellery. There was nothing flashy or obvious about Ada.

'He's not answering,' Simon shrugged. 'I've left a message, saying we don't know how late we'll be. I've said that we've gone off on an adventure . . .'

'That's what it really feels like, doesn't it?' Winnie grinned.

'Are you sure you want me coming along, too?' Kelly asked awkwardly. 'I feel a bit out of place . . .'

'Rubbish,' Winnie said. 'You're as much a part of this as any of us.'

Outside the hotel it was dark by now. The sky had swirled

deep blue and purple, like poster paint and glitter dropped into a jar of water. Snow had begun to fall in earnest, and the teatime shoppers were pulling up collars, winding on scarves and hurrying their pace. Some of them slowed to stare at the sleek, bulky form of the Rolls Royce Silver Ghost that floated to a halt at the main entrance of the King's Arms. The car moved almost silently on the thin carpet of snow. Its engine purred softly, and it arrived like something out of the distant past.

Ada headed towards it as if it was nothing special. It was just her wheels, her way of getting about. Eric was waving out of the window at them, his hands firmly on the steering wheel, looking ruddy-faced, avuncular. He hurried out, bustling up to Ada, stopping to take her arm as she made tiny steps towards the car.

'My,' said Winnie. 'This is the high life, isn't it?' She tutted and blinked up at the falling snow, hoping that all the passers-by would notice her getting into this limousine. 'I feel like I've won some kind of competition . . .'

'Stop your blethering, woman,' called Ada, now installed on the back seat. 'Get inside here. I want to go home!'

He couldn't stay inside the bungalow. Not for much longer. Not for this evening. He'd been stuck in there for days on end and, now that he was on his feet, he felt how oppressive it was. He felt like the magnolia walls were closing in on him. Even with a good number of the books now gone. (Don't think about that. Don't let her make you feel guilty. It had been the right thing to do.) Even with some space opened up now, the place still felt tiny and cramped, oppressive and dark.

He pulled on his long, herringbone coat. He'd sent himself a bit woozy, in that stuffy atmosphere, wolfing down cans of lager, standing by the fridge. He'd spilled beer froth down his coat, but he'd knocked the edge off his thirst and that was when he'd decided he was going out.

Not off down the Legion. Though that would be easy. Sitting with the old cronies, as Winnie called them. Talking the same old rubbish in safe surroundings. But he'd have to explain to them why he'd been away for a week. He'd have to say why he'd been lying down all that time, coughing away, having Winnie look after him. They might laugh at him, or commiserate with him, or – worse – they might even treat him like an invalid.

He didn't want to go to the Legion.

When he was out in the street he found that it was dark, and the yellow sodium lights made the road sparkle buttery gold. The chilling wind plucked and seized at his clothes and the cold went straight into his bones. It was snowing and the flakes were shooting off in all directions, which was disorienting to the old man. He made his way, confusedly, towards the town square. He realised he was holding something in his hand, inside his deep coat pocket. He remembered: Winnie's membership card. He'd brought it out with him. Her membership of the place where she felt at home, like he did down the Legion. Well, that's where she was, was it? Even in all this blizzard? This blizzard that felt like being inside someone's raging headache? Even in this she was out and about, dressed up smart. Well, he would have to see about that.

Those kids at the phone box were calling after him. He felt the impact of a snowball on his back – *whumpf* – against his billowing coat. They were laughing at him and yelling crude names, just like Simon reckoned they did to him. The wind whipped away their voices then and he couldn't quite make out what they were shouting. Stupid kids, hanging about outside a phone box, on a day like this.

Ray found his way to the meagre shelter of the bus stop. It was perspex-sided, vandalised, and the seats there were those flip-down bars that were more hazardous than comfortable. But he was happy to have a sit-down as he waited for the bus to Kelly's town.

Later, as he watched the snowstorm intensify, sitting warm and safe on the bus, he momentarily forgot where he was meant to be going. He shook his fuddled head to clear it and he almost panicked. He looked around himself, at the other seats on the bus. He was the only passenger aboard. Who else would think of coming out today? The driver was taking the treacherous country roads very carefully, bringing his single passenger closer – very gradually closer – to his destination.

And the old man remembered then, where it was he had wanted to get to. The address on the grey card in his coat pocket. The Great Big Book Exchange. That's where he was going to now.

Ada's car moved swiftly and surely through the storm, towards the coast. It was a long journey to make in such conditions, but to those sitting in the back, on the spacious, grey leather upholstery, it was as if the weather out there didn't touch them. They could barely feel the wheels beneath them, touching the frozen road. They didn't get a hint of the bitter cold out there. In the warm, dry belly of the silver beast, it felt like they were flying.

Ada had gone quiet now. She was conserving her strength after her public appearance this afternoon. Once, she had called out to Eric, who was happily chauffeuring them along. 'We did OK, didn't we, Eric? We put on a good show?'

'Yes, of course you did,' he laughed. 'You always put on a good show, old moo.' Ada had looked satisfied then, closing her eyelids and Simon had marvelled once again at her daring in sporting silver eyeshadow.

Winnie, Kelly and Simon went quiet, too – watching the dark, dramatic hurly-burly of the storm, and then the thrashing of the sea as they pulled closer to the coast and hemmed along the cliff tops towards Ada's home. They were content to surrender themselves and go along inside her life for a while.

This day will never end, Simon found himself thinking happily, drowsily in the false heat of the limousine. This day will just go on and on for ever.

After a while, Ada's piercing eyes were open again, alert and fixed on her three guests.

'I'm looking forward to seeing your house, Ada,' said Winnie. 'I'll bet it's beautiful, isn't it?'

Ada sighed. The breath rattled in her throat. 'I'll be embarrassed, to tell you the truth, Winnie. Oh, it's beautiful, by anyone's standards. It's rich and expensive and all of that. But it's a hoarder's house. A silly, vain, rich old woman's house. I've spent my time amassing all this stuff. All this . . .

tat. Just you wait and see. But what good has it done me, eh?' She coughed miserably.

'Nearly there,' called Eric, with a little laugh. He chortled, thought Simon. That was the perfect word for the way that Eric laughed.

'I've spent my life hoarding *things*,' Ada said sourly. She glanced, almost shyly, at Winnie. 'And it's people I have left behind. People like you, Winnie.'

Simon sensed a shiver going through his gran. They were approaching some tall iron gates, which were beginning to open automatically at the approach of the Silver Ghost.

'Do you feel like you've wasted your life, Winnie?' Ada asked urgently, and more quietly. The car wheels were crunching on the snow and gravel of the long drive up to the house. 'Do you feel like you've lived your life doing all the wrong things? Collecting up all the wrong things?'

Terrance was having a quiet day at the Great Big Book Exchange.

No one came by, but he didn't mind. With his jazz playing and all the lights turned just so, and the shadows of the falling snow scrolling through the rooms, he was having a perfectly relaxed day. He brewed up coffee, he nibbled dark chocolate, he flipped through an ancient, outdated atlas of the world. He did everything as he liked to – unhurried, unflustered. When he could go at life at his own pace, it didn't bother him that he had two plastic arms. He hardly noticed. When there was no need to hurry, even fiddly things were manageable: flipping over the Miles Davis LP and putting the needle onto the vinyl; stirring ravioli in tomato sauce with a spatula on the hot plate and eating it straight from the pan. With time, skill, patience, all things became possible.

Terrance spent his lonely Friday in daydreams. He pictured Winnie and Kelly and Simon at their lunch today, all festive and celebratory, wildly applauding the famous author. He tried to imagine Winnie's pleasure this morning, when she'd opened his parcel of books and read his message. He was going back, he knew, on all the things he'd once said, and once insisted upon. He'd tried to impress on Winnie the need to give books away and to return them to the Exchange. Yet now he was urging this whole collection on her: Look! Here are fifteen novels for you to keep for ever. I want you to treasure these, and never to part with them and always to think of me when you look at them or read them.

That was the nature of presents. You kept them in the giver's stead. They were a small part of that person for you to keep.

He found himself longing to dance with Winnie. How

strange. Dancing was something he had never imagined doing for years. Something about her brought out everything quaint, old-fashioned, gallant in him. He wanted to be at a tea dance with her, shuffling and counting steps, one-two-three, on a parquet floor; as the mirror ball sparkled and sent roving dots of brilliance drifting down. Terrance imagined holding Winnie in both his arms – his arms going round her back as they danced close, cheek to cheek. But he would have no feeling in his arms, would he? They would be lifeless, as usual, no matter how much he longed for them not to be. He'd never really touch her, would he? Not really.

What was that?

A great clatter at the front door of the Exchange. The huge whoosh of wind, like a frightened gasp, as the door flew open. It was a gale by now, sucking out all the warmth of the shop's interior, and bundling in . . . who? A stumbling, shambling figure in a scruffy greatcoat. He was wrestling to get the door closed behind him, the newcomer.

Terrance sighed and went to tend to him, wishing he'd locked up already. It was too late for customers, too late for visitors. But now he had one and he'd better see what he could do for them.

The old man was florid, desperate, out of breath. The snowstorm had just about battered the life out of him.

'You'd best sit down . . .' Terrance began.

The old man's eyes were blazing, wild. 'She's here, isn't she? You've got her in this place with you, haven't you?'

Ada accepted all of their compliments with a shrug of her tiny shoulders. As they went through the large, echoing rooms of her home she shuffled ahead, leading the way, looking nonplussed, looking quite at home. She was dwarfed by all the tall doorways, antiques, objets d'art.

Her guests lagged behind, oohing and aahing as if they were on a private tour of a stately home. Their feet tapped loudly on the vast marble floors and Simon was blushing, for some reason. He tried to move very carefully, quite sure that he would knock something over in his nervousness. He would destroy something priceless: this vase, this statuette.

Room after room. It seemed that Ada's house went on for ever, deeper and deeper into the cliff face. It was a series of complicated, luxurious tentacles, tunnelling far into the earth. Its turrets and towers made it look like a palace, Simon thought: it should have been gilded and encrusted with emeralds and rubies, so that it shone in the darkest of nights. It was a beacon, up on that cliff top, staring out to sea.

'Oh, Ada,' he heard his gran say. 'I never dreamed it would be as grand as this.'

They filed through dancing rooms, music rooms, reception rooms, games rooms. It seemed that Ada had brought them the longest way round, to show off how many rooms she had. They passed through a library and even Simon and Winnie gasped. Even Kelly – who was quite used to the Big Book Exchange – was amazed at the sight of those shelves going up to the ceiling. There must have been thousands of books there. Too high to see – much too high to clamber up and fetch down. Books that nobody had touched in decades.

'See?' said Ada. 'I hoard things. I keep them safe, here, all to myself. How useless! How ridiculous! What's the point? If no one can read them?'

'This place is wonderful, Ada . . .' said Simon, in a hushed tone.

'It's a mausoleum,' Ada said. And at last they arrived at the kitchen, deep in the heart of Ada's mansion. It was modern, but homely and comfortable, with a broad table of old wood, where Ada immediately took up position, amongst a nest of scribbled-over papers and opened books and blotchy pens.

Eric was waiting for them there. Somehow he had arrived in the kitchen ahead of them. He was being the perfect, bear-like host: popping on a pinny, opening bottles of wine and asking whether they felt like something to eat . . .?

'Oh, I'm sure I couldn't eat a thing,' Winnie said. 'That lunch was huge.'

'Eric is a fantastic cook,' Ada said. 'He tends to cook things that are too rich for me. It's very good though, if you like that sort of thing.'

Eric stood waiting in his pinny.

'Maybe later,' smiled Winnie. Her face fell suddenly. 'Actually, I'm a bit worried about my Ray. He won't have eaten this evening. He'll have looked at all the weather. It might have panicked him, us still being out in the snow . . .'

'I'll try him again on the phone,' Simon said. He moved away to the window, which was a huge plate of glass filling the whole of one wall, offering a spectacular view of the sandstone cliffs; the black sea and the snow tumbling down, showing no sign of stopping.

Ada had started flipping through papers as her guests settled down with glasses of wine. She was reading things, making corrections, signing her name. She was also catching her breath back, after the walk through the house. 'I'm tying up loose ends,' she told Winnie. 'Like I say, I'm not a well woman. I have to sort things out. I don't want things left messy at the end.'

Winnie looked flustered and embarrassed.

'That's why it's good we've met up again now,' said Ada.

'Right at the end. It's only right. It's . . . symmetrical. You were with me right at the beginning of everything, too.'

Winnie burst out: 'So . . . Are you really dying?'

Ada laughed and wound up coughing. 'Sooner rather than later, I think. But not tonight, anyway. Don't worry.' A look of impatience crossed her alert and pouchy face. 'Eric? Where's my special drink?'

'Here, my sweet old moo,' he burbled, sliding it deftly in front of her.

'I've tried to tell you, she isn't here. She hasn't been here all day. Saturday is her day for coming here, not Friday. Anyway, she's off today, seeing an old schoolfriend. She's gone to have lunch. Didn't she tell you?'

Terrance was attempting to talk rationally to Ray, but could see that his calm, measured speech was having little effect. The old man was working himself up. Terrance could smell the cheap lager on him. There was a manic gleam in his eye, too – and a sinewy, bristling strength to his skinny old limbs. For just a moment Terrance felt menaced by this old man.

It hadn't taken Terrance long to realise who his visitor was. He had arrived shouting and cursing Winnie's name, wanting to know who had spirited her away. Blaming Terrance for turning her head, giving her ideas.

'She's not been right for weeks,' Ray was ranting. 'Coming here. Mixing with strangers. Anyway, what do you mean, "old school friend"? She hasn't got any friends. She's never had any friends in years. She's never needed to have friends.'

'Never needed friends?' said Terrance, astonished. 'How can she not have needed friends? I'd have thought the very opposite was true. She thrives on company and conversation. What, are you saying it's been enough, for her to be just with you? Being your wife?'

Ray's face went dark.

'You think that's enough?' Terrance laughed hollowly. 'You've been keeping her prisoner, man.'

'Don't talk to me about my marriage,' said Ray. 'I'll not have it.'

'It's you who've kept the two of you locked up. It's sheer brutality. And what you did to her books . . .' Terrance shook his head disgustedly. Now he was losing his temper. 'Burning them! Like the Nazis did! That's barbarism.'

Ray took two steps forward. 'What did you call me? I'll have you know I fought a war – aye, I'm older than you – I fought a war against the bloody Nazis. And not so that I could be talked down to by the likes of you. You big nancy wife-stealer.' He pushed Terrance hard in the chest. Terrance was taken by surprise. He fell back a step, winded, knocking into a bookcase. Ray stepped forward again, intimidatingly close; his breath rank; panting into Terrance's face. 'Go on then, man. Punch me back. Go on. Take a swing. Oh, I forgot.' He laughed harshly. 'Armless, aren't you? Completely armless.'

Never had Terrance felt more vulnerable. His arms hung limply at his sides as Ray leered right into his face. All Terrance could do was talk. 'Jealousy's an ugly thing, Ray,' he said quietly.

'You what?'

'You. Scared I'll take Winnie off you. Scared that she's fallen in love with me.'

'Ah. Rubbish. We've been together years.' Ray swallowed thickly, his eyes wild and scared-looking.

'So?' said Terrance. 'Anything can change. Anything at all.'

'Why would she fall in love with you?' Ray sneered. 'You're only half a man. That's all you are.'

Terrance shook his head slowly, sadly. 'I'm more real to Winnie than you are, Ray. Really. Listen to me. It's true. Maybe in the past you were real to her. Not now. *You* are less than half a person.'

'Rubbish.' Ray sounded like he was having an asthma attack. 'You're talking rubbish!'

'I'm missing my arms,' shrugged Terrance. 'But that's just flesh and blood. That isn't all I am.'

'What?' Ray was losing the sense of what was being said to him. Staring at Terrance, he could see dancing motes of light in the air. 'What are you on about?'

'I mean that you aren't even real to Winnie any more. She cooks your food. She sits with you each and every evening. She lies beside you in your bed. But now that she doesn't love you any more, you're less real to her than the characters she reads about. And you're certainly less real to her than me.'

Terrance stopped. He looked at Ray's anguished face, thinking: how can I say such cruel things to him? He's just an old man. An old man who's now got nobody left. How could I be so cruel as to tell him the truth?

'How do you know anything?' Ray shouted. 'Has she said this? Has she told you all this in her own words?'

I could give him a heart attack. It could kill him. He could drop down dead, here in the shop. If I pushed him a bit further. Made him lose his temper a bit more.

'She doesn't have to tell me. I just know. I know what she's thinking, and what she feels.'

Terrance stopped. He waited for Ray to calm down. The old man couldn't get his words out. Terrance had gone too far now. This had to stop.

Ray started to breathe more evenly. The ripples across his vision slowed down.

At last Terrance said, 'The blizzard is worse out there. You'll not get home this evening. You'll have to stay here tonight.'

'I'll not stay here,' said Ray, but by now his protest was feeble.

'There's a chaise longue in one of the back rooms and a rug. It'll be comfortable enough till morning.'

'What? Stay here, with all your dirty old books? In the place owned by the fella who wants to run off with my wife?' Ray laughed.

Terrance pulled away. 'You can do what you want. But that cold out there is perishing. There won't be any more buses tonight. If you go out there, you won't be safe. Is that how you want your story to end? Is that how you want to finish up, Ray?'

Terrance turned and led the way deeper into the labyrinth of book-lined rooms. He was going to make up a bed for Ray, whether the old man wanted it or not.

Ray was surly as he followed. 'OK, then,' he said. 'But I'm not happy. Sleeping among all your nasty, dusty old books.'

'I'm sure,' said Terrance, in an amused tone, 'that we can

find something suitable for you to read. Something to send you off happily to your dreams. As the storm and the night play themselves out . . .'

Still grumbling, Ray allowed himself to be led deeper, into the heart of the Exchange.

'We'll let them talk,' said Simon. He drew Kelly away from the table in the kitchen. Ada and Winnie were in the thick of their memories by now. Stories and more stories were tumbling out; shook out like bolts of old cloth; one on top of another, and each one leading inevitably to the next. Do you remember . . .? And . . . You can't have forgotten . . .?

They were reminding each other of the things they had let slip to the silty riverbeds of their minds. It was as if both of the women had only half a memory each and here, with cries and laughter and talking at full tilt, they were finding a way to restore themselves.

'Why don't you two go and explore?' Eric asked Simon and Kelly tactfully. He slugged more deep red wine into their glasses. 'You should have a good look around this place. Leave those two old birds to it.'

'I don't want to be nosey,' said Simon.

'Oh rubbish,' laughed Kelly. 'He's dying to have a good explore. Thank you, Eric.'

She went off then, leading the way. Simon was amazed by how at home Kelly seemed, wherever she went: even here, in all this luxury.

It was quite late by now. The afternoon had become evening and evening had turned to night and it had been dark outside throughout. Now, with Eric filling their glasses with great regularity, Simon was feeling tipsy.

He caught up with Kelly at the bottom of a flight of cool stone steps. Watery reflections hovered and shimmered in the air, rippling over everything, making the whole cavernous space of the room look magically uncertain. A colossal swimming pool opened up in front of them, weirdly shaped and extending for miles, into the darkened recesses of the basement.

'What a waste,' said Kelly. 'I don't suppose Ada gets to use this much, does she?'

'I suppose not,' said Simon.

Next thing he knew, and without much forethought, the two of them were throwing off their things and jumping into the blood-warmth of the water. Unusual for him, not to have qualms or doubts, or to hang back in indecision. He had a moment of – pants on? pants off? pants definitely on – before he jumped into the pool after Kelly.

As they swam up and down and across and around the

perimeter of the irregularly shaped pool, Simon was revelling in the thought of swimming here, in somebody else's house, without permission, a bit stupidly drunk, with the lights out, with a girl, late at night, warm while the worst snowstorm in living memory battered icily at the coast. It felt wonderful.

Kelly grabbed his leg as he went splashing by. She wrestled him underwater and, exerting more strength than he would have expected, she pushed him up against the side of the pool, against the beautifully patterned tiles, all lizards and sea horses. Her breath was hot and spiced with wine.

'Hey, sunshine,' she said, looming close.

'Hey,' he said nervously. Wow, he thought. Her make-up hasn't run at all. None of it. Not a smudge. Then he was aware that she was pushing up rather closely. He didn't dare look down at her black lacy bra. Suddenly he felt too embarrassed to.

'Simon?' she asked and, very gently, moved in to kiss him. He responded and they kissed gently and then with a little more heat.

Then they drew back, at the same moment, and looked at each other.

'Hm,' said Simon.

'Again?' she said.

They kissed again and there was an awkward, fumbling moment, to do with whose arms went where. Kelly moved back a bit. She looked at him and said, 'It isn't really working, is it?'

He looked down, at the crazily zigzagging reflections on the water. 'Not really,' he admitted.

'It's not doing anything for you,' she said. 'Or me.'

'I want it to,' he started to protest. He heard his voice sounding very young and hollow, bouncing across the cavernous pool.

'Wanting it's not good enough,' sighed Kelly. 'That's all very well. But somehow . . . it's just not there, between us. We've given it a few good tries.' She shrugged and shook out her mane of dark hair, showering him with cold droplets. 'Shall we call it a day, sunshine?' she asked.

After a moment he nodded sadly. 'But . . . what a brilliant day,' he said.

Some time later, towelled off, dressed again, quietly reflective and not at all awkward with each other, Simon and Kelly returned to the kitchen.

They found Winnie and Ada still laughing and chatting. Eric was sitting close by, like a bulky family pet, watching them fondly. Winnie was wiping tears of laughter away.

'Oh, there you are, you two. I hope you've not been up to any mischief . . .?'

They denied it, standing there under harsh kitchen light with damp hair.

'Romance of the year, those two,' Winnie told Ada tipsily.

'Really?' said Ada, raising an eyebrow.

'Oh, yes,' said Winnie. 'They're so well suited. They're both such big readers.'

'Really,' said Kelly, 'there's nothing going on. We're best friends. That's what we are. That's all me and Simon need to be.'

'Oh,' Winnie looked at them. She seemed crestfallen. 'Is that true, Simon?'

He nodded, smiling.

'I was hoping it was something more than that,' said Winnie. 'Really, I was hoping for more.'

Simon shook his head. 'What could be *more* than being best friends? I can't think of anything more, can you?'

Then, soon enough, it was time to go.

Ada had pushed herself too far. After her reading and being out in public that afternoon, she had pushed all her physical resources to the limit, sitting up, drinking and talking and going over the past with Winnie. But it had been worth it.

Simon could see that, in the faces of both these old women, as Winnie bent to give the tiny Ada a hug goodbye. It had been worth it all, to have their reunion today.

Eric was going to drive them home. He assured them that he hadn't touched a drop all night. He was safe to take them home. Through the sheeting, frantic snow, from Ada's front door to Winnie's. The weather didn't bother him. It wouldn't bother the Silver Ghost. They would simply glide through it all, he told them gently. They would glide through the night and through the deadly ice like a hot knife through butter, and soon they'd be safe at home in their beds.

'Come back to see me again soon,' Ada made them promise, waving exhaustedly from the kitchen table.

'We will,' said Winnie, and Kelly and Simon agreed. Then they turned and followed Eric out of the mansion to the Silver Ghost.

They would soon be home.

They relaxed in the back of the car and drowsed there: each swept away in their separate thoughts; none of them knowing yet that, when they got back, they'd find the bungalow empty, the door unlocked, and Grandad Ray gone.

They would panic at first. They would think he'd turned mad and run off into the storm.

But nothing bad had happened to him. It would take till next morning for the weather and the panic to abate, and for Terrance to ring and say that Ray was safe.

It had been a gentle night, all in all, and after all.

The savage, wintry storms had risen up. They had looked prepared to devastate the land. But the dawn came clear. Next morning, everything lay calmly, surprisingly, at peace.

Eighteen

'She told me she was going to do this, you know,' Winnie smiled. 'That night. Back in December. After her reading, when we first met up again. We talked all that night and she kept saying how she had hoarded and amassed all this stuff, all these treasures, all her life. Well, she told me then what she was going to do with them.'

Simon and Winnie were strolling along a broad lane of slate chippings, under the unnatural, bright green of the lime trees. For an hour or more they had been wandering around the grounds of Ada's mansion. It was spring: shoots and buds were starting to poke up everywhere.

'I hope that Eric keeps this place on,' Simon said. 'Who else would be able to afford this? And to keep it up in this condition?'

'Oh, he's going abroad,' Winnie said. 'He told me that at the wake. He leaned down and whispered it in my ear when

284

I asked him whatever would he do with himself now. He said he couldn't bear to live here alone. In this huge empty place. He's going to Italy. And never coming back.'

Simon nodded, turning to look back at the house, and at all the many people milling around the tables set out on the lawns and the drive. It looked like a bit of a scrum back there. It looked like a car boot sale. 'What did you mean, she told you she was going to do this? Give all her stuff away like this?'

Winnie nodded sadly. 'She did. She said she'd have no more use for it. She'd lost all sense of value for the things she'd collected, anyway. So she left instructions, all written down, that Eric was to lay out all her belongings on tables outside their house, and anyone who wanted to could come by and pick up anything they liked the look of.'

Simon nodded. It felt weird and perverse to him. The sight of all those people, hunting and scavenging through Ada's things, unsettled him.

A call had gone out in the local press, and on the TV and radio. All of Ada's many fans were welcome to visit her home today. It was the first time this secretive place had been opened to the public. And they would be allowed to take away a souvenir or two, of the writer whose books they had loved.

'Do you reckon they're all Ada fans?' Simon asked his gran.

She shrugged. 'I don't know. You know what people are like. They love free stuff. But I'd like to think so. She had a lot of readers, you know.' She sighed. 'No more stories. That's an awful thought, isn't it? No more stories from her.'

Simon looked away, out to sea, at the clear skies and gentle waters of the bay, where they had scattered Ada's ashes in February. It had been a subdued, peaceful funeral, after the swiftness and the ferocity of her death. 'It's not fair,' he said. 'The two of you had less than two months to get to know each other again.'

Winnie smiled. 'There's no point thinking like that. It was long enough. We said the things we had to say. We swapped over the few bits of memories, and filled in the gaps and . . .' She sighed. 'We became friends all over again, really. Reassuring, isn't it? Finding out that we're still the same people, all that time later.'

'Poor Ada,' said Simon, as they started walking back to the house.

'She had a good life,' Winnie said. 'There wasn't enough people in it, that's the only thing. The only sad lives are the ones that don't have enough people in them.'

Simon suddenly thought aloud: 'My mum and dad had

people. They weren't lonely. Their deaths were less sad than Ada's, in a way.'

Winnie glanced at him. 'They knew they were loved,' she said. 'And that's the main thing. I hope that Ada knew she was loved, at the end.'

'I'm sure she did,' said Simon, and linked arms with his gran.

Up closer to the house, they watched a local TV news crew shooting a feature on the free car boot sale of the dead author's belongings. The reporter speaking to camera sounded incredulous, that anyone – even rich and deceased – could simply give away what appeared to be rare and valuable ornaments and pieces of furniture. Around him, complete strangers were furtively picking up pieces and examining them carefully. They were still unsure of themselves: still not convinced that they were free to take away anything they wanted.

At one point Eric appeared at the front porch of the house, holding a tumbler of red wine. 'Take what you want!' he roared. 'Take it all away!' And the news crew were quick enough to capture it on tape, before he stomped back into the house.

'He's taken this quite badly,' said Simon.

'He was devoted to her,' Winnie said. 'He was a fair bit

younger, you know. People said he was a gold-digger. But he did everything for her. They were devoted to each other.'

The two of them wandered between trestle tables and realised that the crowds were growing larger, more boisterous as the afternoon went on. They were less inhibited about picking up anything they liked the look of and popping it into their bags. Some cheeky, dauntless souls arrived with hired vans, and could be seen loading rolled-up carpets and fold-down tables into the backs.

Winnie scowled, disgusted by people.

'Everything will vanish soon,' said Simon. 'You should have a look, Gran. You should take something, some souvenir of Ada. She would have wanted you to, you know.'

'Oh, perhaps,' she said, looking like she didn't have the heart. 'We should think about getting home again. Your grandad will fret.'

Simon rolled his eyes. It was strange how, in recent months, his gran and grandad had aged somehow. Since that wild, blizzardy night they had both become more fretful and anxious over the safety and the whereabouts of the other. It was weird to Simon, but maybe that's what being married all that time was about.

These days Winnie didn't talk about being in love with the man from the Exchange any more. It was as if Winnie had decided to settle for the life she already had.

'Books,' said Simon. 'We should choose some books as a souvenir.'

They were confronted by what appeared to be a whole lawn filled with books, spines uppermost, lying end to end on tarpaulins, open to the elements, and exhaling all their must and dust: looking exposed in the brilliant spring sunshine. The books were attracting less attention than all the other belongings. 'Maybe that lot – that rabble – don't think books are valuable,' said Winnie, stooping to see what volumes Ada had kept hidden out of reach in her home.

The only other person there in the field of books was Kelly. At first even Simon didn't recognise her. He hadn't seen her since the funeral, the previous month, and already she had changed. That Gothic black and purple had been dispensed with. Now she was all earth colours, with soft, hennaed hair and a hippyish, tie-dyed green dress, and a lumpy cardigan in orange wool. She was wearing multi-coloured beads around her neck and the biggest surprise was when she turned to smile at Simon and his gran: not a scrap of make-up on her face.

'You look amazing,' Simon cried, as they clasped each other. 'What happened?'

Kelly shrugged vaguely. 'Oh, it's just another disguise, isn't it?' she said.

They wandered along with her through the rows of books. Some of the larger, leather-bound volumes looked ancient and valuable, but here they were lying higgledy-piggledly amongst millions of battered paperbacks.

'Ada was as bad as me,' breathed Winnie.

Simon said, 'She must have spent as much of her life reading as you have . . .'

'I wonder if, somewhere, amongst all these books, I could find the *Children's Golden Annual*.' She smiled. 'That was the book I taught Ada to read with. It was mine and I used it to teach her her letters and everything. It mysteriously disappeared back then and I think she just nicked it off me. I wonder if it's around . . .?'

'It'd be worth looking for,' said Simon.

'It'd take hours searching this lot!' laughed Winnie. 'Still, it's worth remembering. It was all down to me, in a way, wasn't it? I was the one who taught her. I was the one who changed Ada's life into what it became.'

The three of them considered that for a moment as they walked on.

'I'm going to take some books for Terrance,' said Kelly. 'For the Exchange. Nobody else seems interested in liberating them . . .'

'Ada would like that,' Winnie said. 'I told her all about the Exchange. She really liked the sound of it. She loved the idea of keeping the books moving, from person to person, from hand to hand . . . keeping the stories in circulation . . .'

Kelly smiled. 'I'm trying to convince Terrance to go one further. To set some of his own books free. We don't get enough people coming into the Exchange. They get put off, somehow. I'm wondering what it would be like, if we set some of the books free . . . like a flock of doves or something. What if we let loose several hundred novels into the wild air . . .?'

'I've heard about this,' said Simon. 'Where they leave them in cafes and on buses and you pick them up, read them, leave your message and liberate them again, for someone else to find . . . It's like . . .' He smiled. 'Like an even bigger Great Big Book Exchange.'

'New ideas,' said Kelly. 'Terrance will have to be talked into it.' She looked at Winnie. 'He misses you. He says that you never come to see him any more.'

'Ah,' said Winnie. 'Maybe I will soon.'

'He says you've shut yourself up in your house, with your old man.'

Winnie looked annoyed for a second. 'Maybe I decided I had enough books at home to catch up on. I don't need to exchange any just now.'

Kelly nodded. 'Shall I tell him . . . that you might come back some day soon? He'd like to see you.'

Winnie nodded sadly. 'Soon, perhaps.'

They wandered further through the books, stopping occasionally to examine intriguing titles. Kelly was filling an old-fashioned book bag with volumes that caught her eye.

Winnie decided that she wouldn't take any books at all. The resolution came over her all of a sudden. 'It's because of what Ada warned me. She said – don't hoard things. She said – the stories aren't in the books. They're in your head and your memory. The actual books are just where they're kept, in the meantime. She said . . . reading is what sets them free.'

Simon glanced over the field of books and suddenly it seemed like a cemetery to him and each book was a tombstone.

'The books themselves aren't valuable, that's what Ada said,' Winnie mused. 'She said that people and characters and stories are valuable, and it's them we should hoard and look after. Not the objects.'

They all thought about this. A particular edition of

Grimms' Fairy Tales snagged Simon's attention. He plucked it up. 'Personally,' he said, 'I like the actual objects, too.'

'Hm,' said Winnie. 'I'll not take any books. I'll have a dawdle back towards the house. I saw some nice bric-a-brac things that way. Maybe I'll pick up a fancy teapot as a keepsake. Shall I leave you here? And meet up with you later . . .?'

Winnie knew that Simon and Kelly wanted a word alone. He nodded and watched his gran pick her careful way through the aisles of books, across the grass, and back to Ada's palace.

'So . . .' said Kelly, hefting her now quite heavy book bag, and giving Simon an appraising look.

'You look great like that,' he said. 'Less severe. Happier.'

She shrugged. 'So, what are you saying?' She smiled. 'Do you fancy me more, now? Do you fancy me more than you did, now that I look a bit more normal?'

He stumbled, confused. He wanted to tell her that yes, actually, he *did* fancy her more, now that her image was softer, warmer, and she was less like a gloomy fantasy version of herself. But he knew that this hippyish Earth Mother persona was a bit of a disguise, too. Kelly was still making up her mind about who she was.

And so was he.

'It's OK,' she said. 'I didn't change myself in the futile

hope that you'd come running after me.' She gave a laugh, full of bravado. 'Yeah, like that'll happen.' She turned away.

'Kelly . . .'

'I said, Simon – it's OK.'

He hugged the heavy *Grimms' Fairy Tales* up to his chest, almost like protection. 'So are we going to be friends, then?'

'Yes,' she said fiercely. 'That's what we both really want. I want you to be my mate. That's what I need, more than anything. That's what you need, too, Simon. We're both still changing. We're both still finding out stuff about who to be. We're friends.'

He nodded. 'Like Winnie and Ada.'

'Except,' sighed Kelly, 'they were apart all that time. Terrible. They weren't there to badger each other and to tell each other where they were going wrong in their lives. They weren't there to goad each other on. That's what mates do. Only mates are allowed to do that stuff.'

'We won't lose each other,' he said.

'Will you be happy to be that?' she asked. 'My best friend?'

Simon nodded – very happily.

Kelly pointed at the book of old fairy tales he was clutching. 'Are you taking that with you?'

'Hm?' He flipped through the thick pages, examining the

gorgeous, tinted colour plates, kept fresh under slips of tissue paper. 'I think so. A keepsake. I can't believe Gran's gone off to find some old teapot. No, it seems only fitting to take away a book of old stories.' He turned and started walking back towards the house.

Kelly walked along with him, swishing her long skirt. 'Will you bring it to the Exchange, when you've finished reading it?' she said. 'Will you set it free, or will you keep it at home, all to yourself . . .?'

'We'll just have to see,' said Simon.

STRANGE BOY
BY PAUL MAGRS

David's an outsider. He's smart, sensitive – and convinced he has secret super-powers. Life for him and his brother is a constant whirl of would-be step-families and overbearing friends and relations. And even aged ten, he's finding he's not sure what he thinks about fancying girls when 14-year-old John down the road seems so much more interesting...

Paul Magrs' warm, vividly told story of childhood's end blends comedy and drama in a wild play-ground of messed-up lives and family feuds.

ISBN 0-689-83712-7